Of
Green
Illusions

By Clifton Lopez

Order this book online at www.trafford.com
or email orders@trafford.com

Most Trafford titles are also available at major online book retailers.

Printed in the United States of America.

ISBN: 978-1-4120-1464-9 (sc)

Trafford rev. 07/03/2012

 www.trafford.com

North America & international
toll-free: 1 888 232 4444 (USA & Canada)
phone: 250 383 6864 ♦ fax: 812 355 4082

Other books by Clifton Lopez

Lost In Time
  -Killer Species

The Cartographers Line

For *Moises, Joshua, Mikey, James, Dee*
And my family Sheila,
John, Marion, Wilfie
And
Verna Walker — my inspiration.

To Moises and Sheila for their love and support, and John for his love, selflessness and sacrifice, Marion for her love, and Verna for her love and immense patience through trying times. Ken, Donna, Greg and Brian for keeping me laughing.

We shall not cease from exploration

And the end of all our exploring

Will be to arrive where we started

And know the place for the first time.

--T.S. Eliot*

*Lines from "Little Gidding" in *Four Quartets* by T. S. Eliot, copyright @ 1943 by T. S. Eliot; copyright @1971 by Esme' Valerie Eliot.

Of Green
Illusions

He stood on the ledge of the great Cauldarian range looking down at his hand in which he held a rock. The beauty of it was overpowering, its green opaque luminescence made him feel falsely at ease. But he knew this was an object of beauty that no Cauldarian should posses. The stone represented the dark side of their history. The ideological faith and power that emanated from it could also be used for good. But its efficacy was wielded as if it were a sword striking at every aspect of the populaces' freedom. So far, its thrusts proved deadly in every instance. It had to be thrown over the ledge and into the night if his people were to survive.

Michael awoke from this same dream that he had many times before. It was as if it were only yesterday that his world had changed; it was so different, but in many ways, it was still the same....

1

Souvenirs

Michael Norton grew up in a small village on the border of the convergence zone. This thin zone separated the spiritual land were the Cauldarian Gods reined and the land where their disciples lived.

The spiritual area consumed over fifty percent of the arable land on the planet of Cauldaria. The geography of the planet was cut in two halves; one half was unusable to the Cauldarians due to the Gods inhabiting it. The other half was temperate, lush and green. Even though the temperate half of the planet had a lot of tectonic activity and volcanism, it was still a beautiful place to live.

No one knew what was contained in the spiritual side of the planet; they could only use their imaginations to visualize what was there. Only legends passed down from generation to generation alluded to the elusive Gods existing there and the foundations of the Cauldarians faith emanated from these legends.

According to their religious dogma, the spiritual zone was reserved for the Gods and not for mere Cauldarians. Anyone that ventured into the zone would never be seen again, the Gods would not permit the intrusion of lowly beings into their Holy Land.

The beginnings of these legends were thought to have come from the first King of Cauldaria, Keiod. He was said to have journeyed to the spiritual zone and was allowed to enter and experience the spiritual knowledge and faith of the Gods. He was then told to leave the zone to spread the word, take this faith back to his people, and administer it to them as needed. Of course, Keiod would hand this knowledge and faith down to his siblings, to ensure their royal positions throughout time.

The official state religion was to be followed not by choice or by faith, but by decree. Keiod, the first ruler of the unified people of Cauldaria, had created a new belief system that depended upon his autocratic dissemination of the ideas of this new faith to his people. The new religion would reach into every aspect of the lives of the Cauldarians.

Keiod was an extremely powerful ruler; he had control over everything and every thought of his people, as would his heirs.

Even though the Monarchist system had been overthrown for a few millennia, the faith and religion of the first King still endured throughout the land and its many subsequent forms of governing bodies. It was the official religion of the State and no other faiths would be tolerated. The government always realized there was too much power and control in the realm of faith for it to be given to the people to use as their hearts would eventually use it.

The spiritual zone was still a very dangerous place for a Cauldarian. In recent times, a few had tried to journey into the zone for divine knowledge or enlightenment and then suddenly disappeared. There were numerous stories about the government having its hand in their disappearances but no one had taken these reports too seriously.

*   *   *

The planet was in the direct path of the Black Ribbon Abyss. This was a deep space disk of large and small iron, carbon and thibrite compounds. These were caught in the gravitational field of the Cauldarian sun and rotated around it in an almost hyperbolic orbit. It was called the Black Ribbon Abyss because the light from the sun was partially blocked by the rock and dust particles contained in it. In the region where the disk passed between the sun and Cauldaria there was thin darkness. This dark area increased as the planet drew closer and eventually crossed the path of the disk. This occurred at the frequency of four times in the Cauldarian year, which was measured by two complete orbits of the sun. The darkening effect in the night sky was most prominent when the planet was at its perihelion with the sun.

Three moons encircled Cauldaria. Two of the moons: Phobos and Tethys were small as moons were measured. But the third moon Oberonte was in a class of its own. It was two-thirds the size of Cauldaria and with half the mass. It could be considered a planet in its own right.

These three moons were the cause of great destruction on Cauldaria. The gravitational forces on the planet were of the highest order and the tectonic activity of the surface plates was extreme.

This was something they had learned to live with. The scientific community had long ago perfected mathematical theorems and simulations that predicted the planet changing catastrophes before they occurred, so they were always well prepared for the events.

Oberonte was the main source of enormous gravitational stresses to the huge surface plates of Cauldaria, but the large moon was also the planets great protector. Its position at seventy-five degrees south of the equatorial line seemed to protect the lower half of the planet from the meteors when Cauldaria passed through the Black Ribbon Abyss.

The gravitational barycentre of the two celestial bodies would also draw the meteors from the abyss to the area of the planet called the spiritual zone and away from the habitable side of Cauldaria.

There were a few astrophysicists, cosmologists, and astrogeologists that theorized about the nature and composition of the meteors that fell in the spiritual zone. Their radical theories had put most of these scientists in harm's way over the years. The government did not want scientific explanations about the very foundations of the state sanctioned faith that emanated from the spiritual zone.

Most of the scientific theories about the composition of the meteors concluded they were composed of carbonite, iron and thibrite. This was an extremely volatile combination of elements, in more ways than one.

Dr. Thorensen, the most prominent of the Cauldarian astrophysicists, theorized that the heat caused by the entry of these three elements into the atmosphere or an impact combined them to create a new compound. Thorellium, named after himself of course. He thought the new compound would be an extremely hard crystalline rock that would be somewhat clear in appearance and have a greenish color. It would also have a small electrical charge, one that would be unregulated. A small rock would not be hazardous to the touch, but if an area were strewn with them, the electromagnetic field could be strong enough to kill.

Dr. Thorensen also put forth the theory of this is why no one ever returned from the spiritual zone and why the magnetosphere over the zone was so strong it prevented exploration from the air. After the publication of his extremely controversial theory, he mysteriously disappeared.

*   *   *

Michael sat on a small hill next to his house. He was admiring the horizon with its green glow emanating from the spiritual zone that mixed with the early evening sky. Even though he was only a child, he was already fully indoctrinated into the state religion. But he still had questions that he knew he should never ask out loud. His heart yearned for the answers to these.

He watched the heavens and the broken cloud cover that seemed to fill it. The glow from the spiritual zone combined with the sunset to create a greenish blue cloud rack with a hint of purple throughout the sky. The clouds were immense and looked as if they stretched to the stars. The beautiful view had overwhelmed him for a moment. A cool breeze brushed by his cheek as he stared upward.

A sudden feeling had entered him. Michael had never felt like this before, he shuddered. He looked away for a second as he was immersed in this new feeling and then looked back at the evening sky and the feeling grew more intense. He looked at the immense universe lying before him and sensed in his heart there must be some force or God that had created this beautiful thing called life he was experiencing now. He was filled with a deep sense of warmth and serenity.

Michael's heart told him this was God touching him now, a God that he alone had a connection. Some of his questions about life, the universe and his experience in it were laid to rest on this night by simple faith and not by answers that he knew deep down could never be answered by anyone but himself, engulfed within God, in a state of grace.

He knew he would never again believe, as the state would want him to. They would try to excise his new faith, but this was something that no government or no one had control over, especially Michael himself. This was the first time he had felt the virtue of his own true faith in his soul. He finally felt at one with his world and the new spiritual universe that he had communion. He sat there in silence all evening long, until he heard the distant soft voice of his mother calling for him.

With a smile on his face, Michael walked home from the hill with the beginnings of a new understanding of who he was and why he was here.

He would now doubt most of his government's motives and knew he would never worship in the state faith in the future.

Two years later, he would be sent to a state religious correctional school to realign his beliefs with those of the government. He was shocked to learn so many other children and adults had different beliefs as he did. This is where he would meet James for the first time; they would grow up as best friends.

This is also, where Michael learned to keep his true thoughts and feelings to himself. This school would leave mental scars with Michael. These scars were to him, tangible souvenirs he would never lose and Michael, as an adult, would later use these to change his world.

2

Enlightenment

If Our Reach Does Not Exceed Our Grasp,
Then What Is Heaven For?
-- Robert Browning

The building was a huge grayish white block. Its size
was immense. There were no windows, only two
huge doors at one end. As the transport grew closer,
the proportions seemed to increase also. The
transports all had windows, which were later covered
over to hide from the newly arriving students the true
magnitude of the problem in their society. Michael
thought this place could hold hundreds of thousands
of Cauldarians. He was not far wrong.

The emblem over the entrance doors read
"Keiods Enlightenment and Unification Center."
Named after the King who first brought his religion
back from the zone where no one else dared tread.
His religion relied upon divisionism and fear of the
unknown to draw people to the core of the belief

system. Michael understood at an early age these were devises easily used to sway a peoples thinking. It was also convenient, because the King himself interpreted the new creed. Keiod was the great unifier of the early Cauldarian tribes and cultures. He had the ultimate mandate from the Gods to unify his people under one belief system. This would be a system that he would interpret alone. In the early times, if you were a non-believer you did not have much of a future, as death seamed to put a damper on ones futurity.

But these were new modern times supposedly of open minds and no one was put to death for being a non-believer. The general public thought they were confused and needed only to be shown the correct way. And in reality they were thought to be radical and uncontrollable by the government. Because the state religion had its tendrils entwined in so many of the governing systems laws, they felt extremely threatened by these nonconformists. The modern government often used its own interpretations of the theology to gather popular support for an unfair or previously unpopular position.

Michael was still a child, but many would classify him as a young man. His use of debate, positive criticism, and unabashed use of questions on things that should not be put him a little ahead of his chronological peers. He relished in his open-minded approach to the great questions of the universe and nature. "Who are we?" "Where did we come from?" "Where are we going?" "Who or what is God?"

These four questions started his journey to the religious reform school, which he properly called it. Strangely, sometimes he wondered if his self-actuated, so-called open-minded views were just that, self-actuated and not worthy of his contemplation. After all, if everyone else in the world believed in Keiods theology, why shouldn't he. He felt like an outcast from his society.

Then he entered the huge doors of the reform school and his heart could have opened, burst and poured forth love and affirmation to his whole world. It was full, there where tens of thousands of children and adults here with the questions that he had. They may not have been the same questions, but they were questions nonetheless. Because of the incarceration factor, this was not a place where he wanted to be. But it was a place where he had to be To share and maybe find what he was looking for.

The doors closed behind them as all from his transport had entered and were standing in awe at the immense cavern of the central block. For as far as they could see there were small groups surrounding innumerable tables with what looked like a teacher lecturing at each one.

Michael looked back at the huge closed doors once more and thought this may not be such a good thing after all. This would be the last time he would see the outside for two years. He looked to the boy next to him in line.

"Hi, what's your name?"

"James," he replied.

"I'm Michael," he said as James looked away quickly.

He was still looking at James when he felt a sharp pain run across the back of his neck. He quickly crouched down and turned to see what had hit him. It was a large man with an even larger baton in his hand.

The large figure yelled out for all to hear, "Rule number one. Do not speak until you are asked to speak."

Michael had the urge to fight back, but he knew he could do nothing in this situation. He decided then and there to reluctantly conform to all the rules and regulations to hopefully get through this as quickly as possible.

The man then raised his heavy stick at James to continue his objective lesson. Michael thought *damn; I can't conform to this one just yet*. He threw his leg out to trip the large man. It did not work until he threw his arm at him with all his weight behind it. Michael shocked himself; he was a pacifist until now. He just could not let the boy next to him take a beating for answering his question. There was no contest, the man was twice as large as Michael was and knew how to use his body as a weapon. He just got lucky, caught him unawares, and tripped him to the ground. He tried to get the baton out of his hands, but to no avail. The guard struck him with it as he caught his balance. Michaels' left arm cracked with the second blow. He could not fight back. He knew he was no match for him. He thought what a monster, as he heard his bones cracking with every blow. There was no pain yet; just fear and wonderment at how such a Cauldarian could exist.

He beat the young man into physical submission, but as he lay there bleeding on the floor he thought they could do this to my body but not my soul. Through his bloody teeth, he smiled back at his attacker. He knew the guard had taken out all of his anger on him and he would leave James alone. As the pain from his broken bones began to set in, he looked over at James. He could see in his eyes that he had a new friend and a bond that would last for many years to come. He then blacked out from the increasing pain of his shattered body.

Michael and James were from the first, considered non-conformists and were separated from the general populous of the religious reform school.

It had taken months for Michael to recover from his initial beating that he received. The rest of the time spent in the school the reformist teachers would use mental games just short of what a sensible person would call torture.

James was located in the room adjoining Michael's room. The walls were thin and they could whisper to each other during the late night hours. These conversations kept both of them from going insane or worse, accepting the religious dogma of the state. They both decided from early in their incarceration that publicly they would tow the line and agree with everything that was taught to them.

When they were free from their bonds, they would silently live with their previous thoughts and faiths, discard Keiods beliefs, and put the school out of their minds.

*   *   *

Typical group meetings were organized for the teachers to disseminate the religion and to gage their influence and acceptance of it to their pupils. This is where Michael would slip up, because debate and argument was such a basic ingredient of his being.

"Michael, do you believe in the Gods of the Spiritual Zone?" asked the teacher named Brown. "I guess so; I don't know what to believe anymore."

"I would like your thoughts on the subject," as he looked at James.

James replied, "My thoughts have nothing to do with it. It is what I feel spiritually. My spirituality is aligned and is as close to our first kings beliefs as can be." He really wanted to tell Brown to eat shit, but this way he would get out of this hell a little earlier.

"Michael what do you really think?"

James saw it in his eyes and kicked him under the table to remind his friend to hold his mouth. Michael thought that he would use logic in his answer but then thought logic has little to do with faith and especially with the state faith.

"I'll answer you truthfully and honestly. I truly do not see merit in Keiods faith, but I do respect it if you have strong beliefs in this particular dogma. I as an individual Cauldarian cannot tell another that their beliefs are wrong. All I ask is the same respect from you of my creed. My strongest belief is that we are all the sum of our experiences. My experiences are different from yours and yours from mine. I believe that no one person can get the same meaning or interpretation of any religion because of the life experiences we all bring to it. I cannot even begin to relate to you the thoughts and feelings that I receive from my beliefs. I have not the words nor will I ever. They are between me, and what I perceive to be a higher being. I sit here month after month trying to understand your state approved faith and I cannot find a connection to my soul. Believe me, I have tried and tried, but I cannot. I do however recognize and value your personal belief system, even if it is the state faith, because I cannot or have no right to discount the experiences of your life that led you to your conclusion. I believe in free will, especially when it relates to faith and God," Michael explained.

His answer gave him three months in solitary confinement. His only contact would be with a specialist deprogrammer.

James, on the other hand, now played it smart and was treated well by the institution. After a year and a half, he received his realignment of faith papers. He was released before Michael, although his underlying hatred of the school/prison almost surpassed that of his friend.

Michael felt a certain sorrow for the teachers of the school and wondered if they all believed along the same lines as Keiod did or were just doing their mundane jobs.

On the last night of James confinement, the two friends would stay up all night whispering of their thoughts, fears and wondered of the future.

James asked Michael, "What do you dream of doing when you grow up?"

"A few years ago it was to travel and share my beliefs with others, but now it is to fly great ships through the air and into space."

"Why?"

"Freedom," he replied in one word.

*   *   *

Michael would finally learn to curb his mouth and keep his true thoughts to himself. He figured he would be an old man before they let him out if he did not. His new strategy of silence and perceived conformity proved right, he would be released half a year after James.

The two large doors opened and a transport full of new students of faith entered. He looked at them with awe and with pity. He felt awe of what they must be thinking and feeling in their hearts at this point in time. And pity for what they would go through in the next months or years because of it.

He walked through the doors, smiled at the guard who had beaten him two years ago, turned his head away, and looked up at darkening sunset sky. He saw the heavens and the blue stars of the Vernacaria cluster shining through the waning light of the early evening. He stood there and looked up as if for the first time.

Of Green Illusions

3

Logic Gates

It was a beautiful morning; the third meteor shower of the year left in its wake an electrifying feeling in the air. Michael thought of going back to sleep as he rolled over in his bed and watched the view from his window, but a strange feeling of impending turmoil wrestled within his mind. He could not shake it, no matter how hard he tried. He decided to stay awake and lie in bed for a few moments. At least the morning atmosphere would make his trip to work a little more intriguing. Maybe the peculiar feeling he had would then manifest itself.

Michael thought the picturesque green sky would be interesting to watch from the cockpit of his ship on his next few transits to the geostationary platform where he worked as a shuttle pilot. He dearly loved flying and he could hardly wait to set foot on the orbital station, but he wished the flights would last a little longer for the next few days, because he knew they would all be visually spectacular.

"Well," Michael whispered, "since I'm up I should get a bite to eat or it will be a long hard day for me. I will get George to cook up some leftovers. It's a little easier than making something from scratch myself, especially after the long hours I put in last night." He looked around and felt silly for talking to himself. Although, he was not really talking to himself, George heard him.

George was Michaels live in butler. He had to be live in, because George was not a Cauldarian. He was an automated being, a nice way of saying he was an electramorph robot. Actually, he was his only living family, albeit an electro-chemical one.

George was not any run of the mill version from the factory. He was special. The electramorph was integrated throughout Michael's large house. Every room had a central pod from which George emanated. While sitting on the pod he took on what looked to be the form of a soft blob of mercury with a bluish hue. This halo effect around his body was the product of a positive electrical charge that pulsed through his matrix. Through internal electrical and external sound wave pulses delivered by sonic wave inducers imbedded in the walls George would take his hard form, any form that was needed, for any purpose.

The pods were the living outlets for Michael's personal home computer. The computer was the intelligence behind George and was so sophisticated it had some semblance of being sentient.

He was the latest model out of the automation works. It was a production facility that manufactured all sorts of automated robotic machines and so called beings. They were considered a marvel of their technical society, but the governments' artificial intelligence committee had imposed certain limits on the electramorph manufactures association. The committee wanted to limit the intelligence levels of these beings. They did not want them to come close to or rival their flesh and blood Cauldarian masters. Their recommendations were many and were hard to work around for the robotics engineers.

Michael found these delimiters to be an interesting challenge for him to change. He wanted his butler friend to be capable of carrying on an intelligent conversation and most importantly he wanted to give George the gift of humor, although humor was a tall order for a robot.

Electramorphs used countless soft jelly like electromechanical junctures called logic gates. These were similar in function to Cauldarian brain synapses. They all connected to each other through an electrochemical process activated by an electrical pulse. These junctures were always closed and only opened when a query was asked of one. For instance when a basic instruction set was asked, it would connect with another appropriate logic gate to complete its task. An instruction could be as basic as the question of two plus two, which would only need the use of four junctures to answer. On the other hand, to try to answer the supposedly unanswerable abstract question of existence: whom and why we are here would take all of its three-kelatrillion gates to be functioning perfectly. Passing processed information back and forth trying to at least to take a fledgling guess at this inexplicable theological question.

The use of regulated logic gates limited any chance of free and random thought. So of course, Michael had changed George's program to exclude the use of logic gates as designed. He compiled a small program and added it to George's basic instruction set. The program only added ten lines to the code. Three of which read:

1. Logic Gates- (Open, Close) at will.

2. Logic Gates- (Open, Close, Transfer) when asked: What, When, Why, Where.

3. Logic Gates- (Open, Close, Retain) for memory.

Another six lines were used to allow multiple gates to be open or closed at the same time, not in sequence, for random and critical thought. The last line of the code was used to load Michael's little program before the factory installed program initiated.

This opened a completely new world of learning and thought for his electramorph friend. However, this morning George only took the simple form of a Cauldarian cook to help Michael make breakfast.

"What do we have to eat in the cabinet?" Michael asked.

George replied, "We don't have much edible food left. You haven't visited the food dispensary lately." He then located the last piece of food in the house. It was found in the cabinet marked fresh on his fiber bin. It was not fresh.

"It looks pretty disgusting whatever it is. I think I'll just have a drink," Michael indicated. "Wonder if I have a clean cup around here?"

George answered him by finding one in the washing receptacle and remarking, "I wish you would reinltiate my cleaning support program "

"I closed that program because of your constant badgering to be more thoughtful and clean up after myself. Well, I'm trying and you still complain." George looked on with an understanding demeanor as he listened to the dull drone of his friend.

Desperately needing a drink, Michael looked at the cup. Not too clean, but it would do. At least he could not see anything moving in it. He looked at it a second time, just to make sure.

"That was a nutritious glass of water," he grimaced, "at least whatever was on the bottom had the decency to look dead while I drank from it."

George shook his head back and forth in disbelief at his bachelor ways. He would wait until tomorrow and ask again if he could do the mundane chores around the house such as cleaning the dishes and preparing meals. These things were seldom done because Michael rarely had time to do them. George considered doing them behind his back, but then thought he shouldn't because that would break the bond of trust between them. One of his many endearing qualities was his unlimited patience. He knew his help was needed and he would eventually get these duties back. He would wait until Michael realized it.

Michael told George, "I'd better find a clean flight suit or my crew will be upset today. I know there is a clean one around here somewhere. Maybe I'll let you help clean things around here again. I'm just too busy."

George gave Michael a look as if to say, what took so long. "The one on the floor looks clean," George indicated with a slight grin.

Michael gave it the old smell test. "Whoa, this one is ripe!" Michael whined. The wince on his face made George's smile grow wider. He was learning humor slowly but surely. He put the smelly thing back in the "to do" pile of clothes.

"This isn't right," he whispered as he looked at his dirty clothes on the ground. He then remembered there was a clean suit in his flight bag. He went to the closet, pulled out the well-worn bag, and looked in it.

"Yes," Michael yelled aloud as he clenched and shook his fist at his live in butler, "I found a clean one, no lonely bachelor jokes from the co-workers today."

He thought about being called this and how long that tag would stick with him. Actually, how much longer he could stand not being with the love of his life.

George looked quite perplexed; he did not understand the emotional intricacies of love or the lack of it. He thought about asking for an explanation, but decided not to. It seemed that at this point no one that came in contact with him knew anything about it. They all had their troubles at one time or another. He thought that is one area, where an electramorph should not tread.

All of the rummaging around looking for clean clothes had made Norton hungrier than he was before. He fumbled with his clothes as his stomach growled and found something bulky in the chest pocket.

"What's this?" he asked as he looked at George. "This is my lucky day, a big juicy energy bar. This should keep me going until tonight."

He started to eat the bar and almost choked as he begun to laugh. *What if, I also had to find a clean pair of underwear? Then I would have been in a fix.* Luckily, the flight regulations prohibited the wearing of under-garments because of the temperature management of the flight suits. *The past Kings of Cauldaria never had it so good, no underwear and a full belly*, he thought to himself as he laughed. George looked on and wondered why Michael was humored so at eating an energy bar. He decided not to ask, because he still had only a limited understanding about the concept of Cauldarian humor and its strange limits.

It was getting late in the morning. George asked Michael, "Shouldn't you be leaving soon? If not, you won't arrive at the ground station on time."

George was also, among many other things, Michael's unforgiving alarm clock. Michael thought he was just trying to get rid of a pain in the ass.

"OK George, although my flight has been scheduled for a late ascent, I'll be on my way."

He looked out the window before leaving and gazed at the enchanting sky. In addition, he realized the meteor showers and the electrostatic interference they produced would make his job a little more difficult over the next few days. Most Cauldarians were happy with the beautiful showers. Even though he also loved their sight, they were demanding on him and the shuttle crew. The needles on the shuttle instruments would be doing a dance all during the flight because of the electronic anomalies in the atmosphere.

His copilot James would most likely be on edge, because he was easily disturbed when their flights did not proceed exactly as planned. James was somewhat of a control freak and Michael was going to have a good time screwing with his mind in the shuttle cockpit during the showers. He acted as if he didn't care when things did not work properly or when he was purposely goaded, but everyone especially Michael could tell that he did care. The signs were quite noticeable. Among the many symptoms were his lips. They would start to turn purple and quiver at both ends as his blood pressure began to rise. The thought of his friend's reaction put a mischievous smile on his face.

"Well, I guess it's been a pretty good morning," he thought, "I've found a clean flight suit and breakfast. What else could anyone ask for?"

Michael stepped out of the house and found the encompassing sky to be one that could only be matched by the ones in his dreams. It was magnificent and he could almost feel the warmth of its color against his skin. He somehow had a sense this was one of those surreal views and feelings that he should put in the back of his mind and lock away to remember someday. The magnificent sun and moonrise was an ideal vista for him to daydream about this morning. He had a penchant for musing about science and philosophy during moments like this.

He remembered his youth and the mornings spent fantasizing while watching the sky. He thought about the universe and its many undiscovered diverse occupants and their societies and wondered if out there somewhere there was another little boy looking up at the sky and dreaming as he did.

These were only his childhood dreams, but he thought they were the best of his earliest memories. He reached out with his mind and imagination and dared to wonder. They were as a young boy the most innocent of dreams for Michael, but they were not for others of his society. They were the most dangerous thoughts that a Cauldarian could have. Thoughts of this type were foreign to his people's culture. Their heritage and belief process would not allow them to fathom such ideas, except in the innocence of a young child's mind. Even then, they would be expurgated if espoused too vocally. However, this morning he was a man and he took great pleasure in these warm feelings and the meshing of his childhood memories with those of his current senses.

4

Innocence

Michael decided to stop by James' place. To see if he wanted some company on the way to the ground station as he usually did. They both seemed to enjoy their talks on the way there. He was in a good mood because of the unusually beautiful atmosphere. He also seemed to have a strange but happy giddiness during the short drive and was already thinking of things to talk about when he arrived. He of course thought the bulk of their conversation would be about the weather.

As he drove up he noticed James' driveway was littered with broken pieces of furniture, garbage and paperwork blowing about. This was curious as his friend was a perfectionist and cleanliness was one of his highly valued virtues. He thought about not disturbing him, but then decided that he should find out what was going on or see if he needed help with anything.

He knocked at James' entryway. A few seconds later, the automatic door opened for him.

"Never did trust these damn things," Michael whispered under his breath.

After getting whacked a few times by his own door, he relinquished his nifty device to the great Cauldaria abyss. It was commonly known as the garbage dump. Jumping past James' door he walked into a room that he had not seen before. He had been in his friend's house many times before, but it had never looked like this. There were papers strewn about everywhere. Cushions on the floor, computer equipment dismantled and all of his furniture had been turned over.

James walked out of the family room and into the living room where Michael stood. He looked disturbed. As if, he had been in some kind of altercation. He was wondering what happened, but not wanting to be intrusive with him. His copilot friend was the type that did not take readily to questioning. Although, he was still curious about what happened.

I will try not to put him on the spot, Michael thought, *I will make a joke out of it.*

"Hi James, you must have had some wild party last night. You should have invited me, your good old friend. I would not have made such a mess of your house. Is everything all right partner?" Michael said smilingly.

He looked back at Michael as if he wanted to say something important, but then shook his head and said, "Yeah, the party I had did get a little out of hand."

Michael thought to himself, *I guess he decided to take the out I gave him.*

"I'll be just a few moments." James wearily indicated.

They both decided to take James' new tram to work. It was faster and they wanted to break it in. He had the typical pilot vehicle. Most pilots had fast means of transportation that emulated their hazardous profession. The shallow cultural viewpoint that most Cauldarians believed was that they were all vein. The truth behind the matter was most of the fast-mover or orbital pilots needed the adrenaline rush. Their personalities craved it. James was not one to break this tradition. His tram was of the fastest line that was manufactured.

Michael really wanted to get his hands on it. But as the pilot of his own new high-speed ship he understood that any self-respecting pilot hated riding in the co-pilot seat of his own vehicle, especially the overpowered dangerous ones. The distinction here was "overpowered and dangerous" vehicles. Most pilots did not mind being flown or driven around by ordinary means, but when it came to perilous velocities most wanted to sit in the command seat. Therefore, as the ever-diligent friend, he decided not to ask.

On the way to the Central Command ground station, he noticed James was apprehensive and not very talkative even after a little prodding. This uneasy quiet was an unusual state for both of them. They usually had the problem of each getting a word in while the other ran off the mouth.

As the captain of his own ship, Michael had the authority to ground any of his crew if they were acting strange, for any reason. But he thought he would let James slip by today. Something was wrong and as his friend, he decided to give him the space and the time to sort it out. He could always handle the ship by himself if need be. He hoped this decision would not come back and haunt him later in flight or on the space station.

Michael never knew this would be the last flight he would make with his friend or the last time he would think of his childhood dreams as innocent.

5

Journey

There was no conversation between the two as their tram climbed the Cauldarian mountain range that lay before the plateau where the launch facilities were located. It was an odd silence. Both wanted to talk, but neither of them knew what should be said to start the conversation. They stared ahead, both feeling uncomfortable.

The tram broke over the crest of the mountain. On the other side, caught in low orbit was the Cauldarians second of three moons. It seemed to float just above the plateau horizon looking as if it were a great celestial ball searching for a place to rest. Its larger sibling moon, already at its culmination, rested above and to the right. It was casting a giant purplish blue shadow on its little orbital companion. This combined with the green meteor showers currently streaking through the sky, made them both look at each other as if to confirm the beauty that set above the horizon before them. They both muttered at the same time, "Wow!"

It had taken the splendor of nature to break their verbal impasse. James noticed a tiny glimmer of light, a reflection, in the sky just between the two visible moons.

"It sure is strange to think that by tonight we will be walking around in that little flicker of light." He was talking about the space station. From their standpoint, it was just a pinprick in the sky. But up close the station revealed its great size. It had accommodations to hold the population of two large cities and all of their auxiliary functions.

"Yeah, sometimes it takes me aback, how I can be standing here on the surface of Cauldaria and later in the day be in orbit, walking on the space station and looking down at the spot where I was thinking these thoughts," Michael replied.

"Pretty neat, huh?" James said, looking for conformation.

"Yup."

They both had the look of wonderment on their faces. "James, stop the tram. I want to take this in for a moment." James did what was asked and was glad. He too enjoyed the view.

They both exited the vehicle and stood leaning against it. With his eyes fixed on the sky above him Michael almost fell as he momentarily forgot about his balance as he craned his head to take in the view of both moons and the meteors. In addition, while looking at the vast distances of space, James unconsciously relied on the only close stable reference available for his own equipoise. Unfortunately, this time out of the corner of his eye, he used Michael. James on seeing his friend leaning uncontrollably for just a split second also lost his balance. They came crashing together, hitting their heads. They looked like idiots and they knew it. They immediately looked around the barren road to see if anyone had seen them perform their clown act. Of course, nobody did and they both broke out in laughter as they rubbed their heads.

Michael looked up at the little speck in the sky again and watched as a meteor streaked by. "That was close."

"What was close?" James asked while still rubbing his head.

"That meteor almost hit the station."

"Yeah, there have been a lot of close misses in the last few days."

"I wonder if any have hit."

"I would bet at least one did," James looked away as he answered his friend.

They both looked up at the space station again and noticed a faint blinking light heading toward it.

"It must be captain Belkers morning supply transport," James said as he squinted his eyes, trying to get a better look.

"No James, look for the strobe lights. Military ships do not have alternating strobe beacons. Do you see any?"

"No, all I see are the red and green position lights."

"That means she's a military vessel. I wonder what they are doing."

"They're probably not on a sightseeing tour," James replied.

"There's another meteor streaking by the station. I sure would like to see one up close. I've always wanted to know what they look like."

James thought, *be careful what you ask for.*

6

Catastrophe and Legend

The high-speed friction of the meteor projectiles produced the green of the showers. They would heat when entering the dense atmosphere. The heat in turn tended to make the meteors explode in brilliant flashes of opaque green light. The friction of the meteors also left long extended green tails as they descended through the atmosphere. The tails sparkled like the stars they fell from in the dark night sky. The particles that separated from the main body where destined to burn a lonely death. They gave an awe-inspiring visual spectacle as they met their demise.

These were only visual observations of the end of the life cycle of the elusive rocks. No living person had ever been close enough to touch one that had fallen or had lived to tell about it.

There were old yarns and great legends on the origins of these rocks and the purpose they held. These were passed on from generation to generation and were usually embellished at every turn. The legends of the green meteors grew over time and their association with the Cauldarian spiritual land only fueled these on.

Early in the quest for space travel there had been attempts to capture the brilliant green meteors during their decent through the atmosphere, but none were successful. The government did not sanction these nor, if they knew of them, would have allowed the endeavors. To avoid them was one of the first rules taught to young and old pilots alike.

One of these early first sub-orbital flights was made in the "Ulane," a new class of ship with enough thrust making it capable of escaping the upper atmosphere and into a lower orbit. Its captain "Jack Soller" now a household word, was on this flight, just as unproven as his newly designed vehicle.

His flight orders never included a planned rendezvous with anything, let alone a meteor. However, the Cauldarian trajectory engineers never thought of or considered entering the calculations of the meteor showers during this first flight. On most of the first scientific experiments ventured in the unpredictable medium of the space, this was one of those little things that usually slipped by.

Young aviator Soller was sitting on the launch pad staring at the switches and dials just in front of his face. He had been looking at them all morning while waiting for authorization to start the countdown. He would then finally flip the ignition lever. He was staring at them so long he started talking to the attitude gyro to break the boredom.

"Hello, little guy. You're going to be nice to me today, aren't you?" It of course never replied, but Soller acted as if it did. "Yes, we will be taking off in a little while. Then you can do your job to help me out," he paused and listened for a few seconds. "No, the ground crew doesn't want us to leave. They're a lonely bunch, but I'm sure they will let us go soon."

Unaware the flight communication line was open Soller kept on until the flight director interrupted him, "OK Soller, we will let you and your little friend go. Start your countdown in five, four, three....

As he flipped the switch to start the countdown sequence, he remarked, "So you heard me huh?"

"Yes, we thought about calling the flight surgeon and having you committed."

"Yeah, I'd be waiting in line behind you guys?"

Once started, the countdown sequence would take two hours and it was completely automated. All Soller had to do was sit there and watch the instrument panel for anything out of order.

"Cauldaria, calling Soller. Come in Soller."

"Yeah, what do you want?

"The next procedure will take some time. The ground control computers will be cross checking with your onboard programs for a while. You can start talking to your ship again."

"Thanks, I think I'll just do that."

The control center and the Ulanes computers were feverishly passing thrust and trajectory algorithms back and forth when the Ulanes ignition cycle suddenly triggered. The computer program had a bug written in it, a big one. At a point in the preflight checklist were the computer was to check the position of the main fuel feed valve, the computer opened it instead of checking it. There was full fuel flow streaming to the engines. At full flow the engines spark igniters automatically lit the mixture gushing through the aft thrust collectors.

Soller was now, albeit early, unscheduled, the captain of a flying vehicle, and was no longer tied by gravity to the ground. There were at least an hour's worth of computations and checking before the flight would be ready to lift off, but she was ascending to orbit now, nothing was holding her back. All of the elaborate trajectory computations were out the window. The captain had taken control of the ship using the manual joystick for attitude adjustments. It was all he could do just to keep his ship in controlled flight, let alone a prescribed course. The Ulanes rocket motors were all firing at full thrust and completely unsynchronized. After locking the fuel valves open for a few moments the automatic program decided it was malfunctioning and made the unilateral decision to shut them all down, while the Ulane was in high ascent.

Soller was just getting his bearings and getting her back into controlled flight when the thrust stopped. The sudden deceleration threw him forward into the seat restraining harness. His arms and legs were flung forward, flailing as if there were hurricane force winds behind him. The instant high negative gravitational forces started to give him the pilot's well-known and feared tunnel vision. Just as he was about to lose consciousness, the forward pressure subsided. He started to regain his awareness and his vision started to return to normal. He was now in a state of weightlessness, floating to be more precise. He had little time to recover, because the Ulane was seconds from falling back upon its ascent track and into an uncontrollable tumbling plunge into the lower atmosphere.

As Soller gathered his wits, he hit the capsule ejection button without thinking about it, almost as a reflex action. The cockpit capsule separated from the main empennage with a blast as the explosive connective bolts detonated. Then the small directional thrusters fired putting some distance between the two free falling hunks of metal.

He looked through the windshield as he turned his small capsule to attain a re-entry attitude and saw the main hulk of the ship he just left behind struck by one of the fabled meteors. A bright green and yellow flash engulfed the Ulane and decimated it. He noticed nothing was left, except a piece of the meteor that had broken off during the collision and landed on the heat resistant window seal right in front of him.

He was in shock. He was closer than any Cauldarian had ever been to one. He thought, *how could I get that rock in here? I have no way of getting it. This would be the find of a lifetime. If I could only....* The little craft started its fall through the atmosphere and all he could do is sit there and watch the increasing atmospheric friction move his rare specimen closer and closer to the edge and finally fall off into oblivion forever.

As Soller gained control of his re-entry, the ground control personnel seemed to be more interested in the rock on the windshield than the procedures of his descending flight. Everyone was watching the video feed from the Ulanes orbital life raft with awe. This was the first time anyone had seen one up close. Everyone was fixated on the large picture screen on the wall. In the meantime, Soller was in the fight of his life trying to keep his flight control system in check and his attitude at an even positive twenty-seven degrees to avoid an uncontrolled acceleration and the eventual burn-up that would ensue. The control center eventually came around and helped him by uploading a number of automatic emergency procedures to his command flight computer. These would take some of the load off his shoulders until he had the landing aerodrome in sight. Upon visual acquisition of the airstrip, Soller would take full manual control of the flight and land without any computer help.

Captain "Jack Soller" was a hero. He returned safely from the catastrophic first flight. He would make many more contributions to the space program throughout his career. But none of his subsequent flights would be remembered like the first one. He gave the Cauldarians the first glimpse of the mysterious green meteors.

There was no physical proof of the encounter. There would only be stories of this passed on as the government immediately confiscated all of the video disks and gave all the personnel involved a non-disclosure, with penalty of death, paper to sign. Nevertheless, they could never stop all of the stories from leaking out. The legends were added to as time went on.

Of Green Illusions

7

The Sarling Plateau

The plateau where they stood was just over the leeward side of the Cauldarians largest mountain range. The area was unofficially named after an obscure scientist named Sarling. It was quite desolate. It was a perfect place for launch facilities. The site was out of the way of the general populace just in case of a catastrophic accident. The desolation of the area was due to an extremely dry and arid landscape. Because of this, no one wanted to live there. It was sanctioned and officially made off limits after the government started the space program. When the land was procured, no one put up much of a fight, except

Robert Sarling, an old and crusty ecologist. Sarling was an eccentric man, about which many stories were told. Most were probably untrue, but he did not mind. If the truth were known, Sarling most likely started most of them anyway.

His champion cause was the government's lackadaisical attitude towards the ethical treatment of other species. It was an easy subject to talk about and to understand, because there were only three other known mammal species still living on the planet. One was a rodent like animal and the other two were domesticated and used as small pets. Luckily, their meat was toxic; probably the main reason for their survival.

Speciesism was one the basic pillars of the Cauldarian psyche. In its earliest history, there was a great abundance of wildlife. All of the different mammalians were known to be very fruitful in the many varying environments of the planet. Then the Cauldarians acquired the taste for dead animal flesh.

Sarling proved, in one of his many books, that the main cause of the extinction of the majority of the so-called lower species was over hunting. The early settlers did not understand the usefulness of breeding food. Therefore, when the local supply of wildlife was exhausted, they simply moved on to other areas. This eventually killed everything warm blooded, specie-by-specie.

The only food supply that survived the early years was plant life. The current society was agrarian not by choice, but by the actions of their ancestors.

Sarling took his arguments of "Speciesism" to another level, a religious one. He put forth the idea that all animals were created from and by God and should be treated as such. He stated, "We should have had reverence for all living and breathing animals, they were all precious, for as they were created from Gods universe, they were part of God. They should have not been killed and eaten for the base pleasure of taste!" After this and other similar statements, he strangely disappeared.

Most thought he was eliminated because of his environmental and extreme Speciesism stances. Others thought it was because of his differing view of religion, which the state could not permit. Few knew the real reason.

He was just about to disclose the findings of an investigation the government did not want published. The Ministry of Health started a secret program. It was performing preliminary tests in the mutation of Cauldarian DNA to grow and produce meat products for public consumption. The doctors took cell-sized specimens from live Cauldarians. They then cultured and grew them in a sterile laboratory setting and then delivered these to a government run processing plant.

The first tests proved too hideous even for the scientists running the program. They grew all the samples to full size. The replication was not exact or not even close. The resultant beings were oddly formed blobs of living flesh and bone.

The Ministries subsequent tries or "batches," as they called them were not taken to full term and did not have any noticeable appendices or markings to remind them of what one was looking at. These also, were deemed too barbaric. The government was correct in thinking its people would not stand for it. The program was canceled and all of its research was buried in secret files never to be opened again.

Sarling was about to distribute his findings with the belief that the disturbing DNA meat production program, was in his eyes, the equal in effect of what they as a collective society had inflicted upon other species throughout time.

*   *   *

They sat on the plateau observing the morning sky like children watching a storyteller. The story they watched this morning had the questions that had been asked for eons. Philosophers of the past and present were not free to discuss their true thoughts because of the government's position and control of the areas that made up their purview. On this morning however, they talked about the basic questions that little children would always ask and would seemingly have simple explanations. The answers were anything but simple.

"What do you think the correlation is between size of the universe and the fourth dimension of time? How are time and the gravity of mass involved in those vast distances?" Michael wondered aloud, "I sure would like to know if there are more than the eleven dimensions explained in the quantum mechanics theory?"

"I don't know, I suppose the only one that could answer that question is the one that made the universe."

"Yeah, it always seems to come down to that reply when the basic questions of nature and the universe are asked. It sure does show how little we know or think we know."

"Ugh, my brain hurts."

"I think I've experienced enough nature this morning. Let's get back on our way."

"That was exactly what I was going to say, Michael."

Of Green Illusions

8

Gravitational Wasteland

The gravitational center between Cauldaria and her three moons made orbital flight in the northern hemisphere almost impossible for at least one fifth of the year. Phobos and Tethys hardly made a difference. Their only influence on the gravitational fields was a slight lateral anomaly in the direction of pull towards the main disturbance between Cauldaria and its largest moon.

Oberonte, the biggest moon, was the real problem for the flight crews of Cauldaria's orbital space fleet. The chemical burning engines of the old fleet simply did not have the thrust needed to escape the oblivion of the "death" field. Its name was unofficially given by the flight crews that skirted around the edges of the invisible force that drew craft toward it and rarely gave up its prey. But the new quantum engines installed on the deep space craft, of which Michaels was one, would not have the problem of the earlier transports, especially like the ones in his early flying career.

*   *   *

As a junior grade pilot, this area was not to be approached and certainly not traversed. But this of course, was just a rule and these yearned to be broken by young aviators that thought they were the best. Nothing could stop a few from trying every year. Some would pay with their lives and some would gain glory, although unofficial and unsanctioned glory.

Michael's first foray into the zone was not made for personal gain or prestige, but for another. He was just finishing his last solo sub-orbital training flight before being allowed to proceed to full orbital flight and receiving his orbital wings when a distress call echoed over the communication system. Distress calls from fleet vehicles took priority on all frequencies and over all com sets. Every ship in the

Cauldarian fleet heard these once one was dispatched. The only problem was that Michael's underpowered training ship was the only one near and under the zone. Other more experienced captains with more powerful ships were at least a half-day away.

"Mayday, mayday, this is Cauld 88329 transport ship. I'm caught in this damn death zone. Is there anybody out there that wants to help an old ship?" echoed the old surly voice of Captain Charles "Charlie" Dunham. He was one of the oldest captains in the fleet.

Michael thought to himself, *what in the hell is he doing in there? He should know better, with all of his experience in orbital flight. He must have eighty years of flight knowledge under his belt.*

Before the flight command center gave a response. The same mayday transmitted again. A young controller at the other end in a trembling voice asked. "What do you need sir?"

Charlie quipped back. "I need to talk to someone who didn't just get off his mommas teat."

There was an odd silence for a few seconds when an older more experienced voice broke in with a reply. "Explain your 'mayday' captain."

"I was dropping sonic mass buoys for the Ministry of Science in the zone. They were to be used in mapping the area for navigation or non-navigation as the case may be," Replied Captain Dunham.

"This is orbital control. You know that no one is allowed in there, for any reason."

Charlie replied in a half laughing and coughing voice. "You're boring me. Check with the director of the Science Ministry. I had clearance."

The controller countered. "Then what went wrong--"

Michael broke in between the two arguing voices on the radio, "This is Cauld 53934 on a training mission below you. From the radar read-back it looks as if I'm the only one in close enough to try a rescue."

"That's what I like, a young pilot with guts." The captain responded.

"My name is Michael. Captain you are the one with the experience. You give me the directions and I'll be there for you."

Captain Dunham's ship was equipped with six extra engines. This gave his ship triple the thrust of the average orbiter. These were to be used to get into and out of the zone. There was also a fudge factor included in the thrust equations incase the captain needed to deviate from the proposed flight plan a little. What the flight plan did not have figured into it was the malfunction and explosion of the thrust nozzles on four of the added engines. This effectively left the gruff old captain caught in the gravitational field between the two large celestial objects with no hope of escape.

Captain Dunham's ship was floating closer and closer to the junkyard. This was assumed to be the middle of the gravitational field due to all of the old hulls gathered there. They just floated there, dead and lifeless, looking as if it were a strange depository for ships of cold hard steel dangling on invisible wires hanging from the cosmos. But they also contained something disturbing in their interiors. Many of them were the coffins of foolish pilots or of their malfunctioning craft. Most pilots who saw this place thought it to be the eeriest of places, including Dunham. He looked out his windscreen and whispered, "Those poor bastards." Dunham felt the hair on the back of his neck stand. He then felt a flush of heat through his body, as he thought, *what if I were to add to this collection of derelicts*. He always had the wish to be buried in space, but he wanted at least to be dead first.

Interrupting his dark and morose thoughts like a welcomed and old friend, Michael's radio call to him for coordinates for a flight path was as uplifting as a new morning's sunrise. Michael punched the numbers he received from Dunham into his navigational unit and up popped the message. Restricted Zone, flight prohibited. Michael wondered, *now how in the hell am I supposed to get into the zone.* If the flight coordinates were not approved the engines would not fire him to the higher orbit to rendezvous with Dunham.

He radioed the captain. "Captain, I just plugged in the numbers and the computer won't authorize the flight there. What should I do?"

The captain called back. "Son, this is your first lesson in the Dunham flight school of how to do things right. Unplug the damn thing. Turn your ship facing my coordinates and flip the firing switch twice. The second time is the override incase the navigation unit fails. That's one they don't teach in the flight program."

"What else don't they teach?" Michael replied.

"It would make your head spin. But I couldn't reveal that stuff." Dunham said with a humorous tone. He knew the controllers were listening and thus the government. He did not want to push his hand too far, at least on an open frequency.

Michael felt a little uneasy at going into the death zone willingly, but he also had a sense of exhilaration of doing something dangerous and against all norms. He thought how many other junior pilots had the chance to do something like this and have it sanctioned as a rescue mission.

He reached behind the navigational console and pulled all the wires, disconnecting and disabling the unit. Then using his small directional thrusters he pointed his training vessel in the direction of Dunham's ship and flipped the ignition switch twice. To his amazement it worked. Michael pushed the throttle lever full forward for one hundred-ten percent power for two minutes to achieve escape velocity. This would allow his ship to go from the training sub-orbital altitude to true orbital capability and headed straight for Dunham and the dead zone.

As he drew closer, his apprehension heightened and he noticed sweat dripping from his brow. He strained to see far off into the distance. The junkyard was ahead. It was just a little dot in the night sky. Suddenly he felt a side swaying motion. The little dot was now heading to the right of his windscreen. He thought his ship was drifting off course due to the strengthening gravitational forces. He looked at the surrounding star field for coordinates and after a few moments of hurried calculations he deduced that he was actually still on course, but the heavy tail end of the ship was swinging around. The aft had the most mass with its heavy metal engines attached. So logically, it would be attracted to the middle of the zone first.

He now had to navigate using the video ports mounted on the sides and the back of his vessel. Michael did not like this type of visual input, because it reminded him of playing video games, and he was lousy at them. He liked the real world and using all of his senses to make his way in it. Although, there was one advantage of using the video screens, it was the digital zoom capabilities of the cameras. He punched in a twenty percent zoom factor and overlaid a crosshair on the screen.

He could not believe it. There must have been close to a hundred ships stranded in the small area around Dunham's ship. Michael could not avoid seeing the captain's transport. His ship was the only one in the quagmire that had every navigational light on and shining brightly. The rest of the ships were cold, dead and lifeless.

Michael called on the radio, "I sure would hate to have your electricity bill."

The captain laughingly replied, "When you get in close enough deploy your grappling hook. It should automatically connect to my ships magnetized forward hull plating."

"That's affirmative captain."

Michaels vessel began to slow down because it was approaching the center of the zones pulling and tugging forces. The accumulated mass of the other stranded ships also contributed to his deceleration, but to a lesser extent than the great gravitational effects of Cauldaria and her large moon.

Just before he passed Dunham's vertical axis Michael deployed the hook and line. Luckily, it made a perfect connection on the first try, because if he had missed, his little training ship did not have enough thrust to reverse itself and go for a second chance. Now both ships were tethered together and held in place with only a small hope of survivability.

"Now what do we do?" asked Michael.

"We're going to put on our space suits, unbolt and transfer the extra unexploded engines to your ship. I'm positive that your light ship with all that thrust can break this bastards grip on us. You do have a space suit onboard?" Dunham replied.

"Yes, captain I do. It is an older model and I don't think it's ever been used. I guess this will be its first test."

"Good, I'll meet you on the tether line." Dunham said in hurried voice.

They spent the better part of twelve hours transferring the engines and Michael was amazed at the older captain's stamina. Michael could barely go on, but Dunham was still going strong when they finished. Dunham went back to his ship to gather up some of the personal effects that he had gathered over his long career. Due to the small weight limitations, it was heartbreaking that he could only bring one small bag back with him. His whole life packed in a little flight bag.

Michael watched from the training vehicle as Dunham exited his ship. He closed the hatch of the transport and made his way across the tether line. Half way along he stopped and turned around to look back at his life's work.

Michael knew it was not just a vehicle to him. Rather than if they were just hunks of metal, most pilots that rely upon their ships during hazardous missions have a deeper connection to them. He respected him and understood it was a difficult time for the captain.

After a few moments, Dunham entered the training vehicle, closed the hatch and strapped into the instructors seat.

As Dunham took off his gloves, he told his young friend. "What a way to end a flying career--"

Michael interrupted, "You can get another ship if you want."

"No kid, I'm done. I have had it with all the government rules, regulations and restrictions, but most of all I am through with all the secrecy. I can't fly under these conditions anymore." As junior pilot, Michael was just beginning to understand what the captain was saying.

They wired all of the engines ignition switches together into one overgrown electrical connection. Looking at each other, they both flipped the switch at the same time. The thrust threw them back in their seats for a full ten-minute burn. They only needed an eight-minute burn to get out of the zone, but they included a two-minute safety margin, as they did not want a similar fate of the others that wandered back there.

They were on their way back to Cauldaria and to a long friendship. Michael now had a mentor in his life that would pass on his wisdom not only of flight but also of how politically; things were done in flight operations within the government. As Dunham always said, "There is the right way, the wrong way and the government way."

9

Oberonte

Oberonte, the largest of the Cauldarian moons possessed a wealth of raw materials. These elements were used for the production of the central governments black or secret projects office buried deep in the Ministry of State. The only thing needed was to build production bases to extract the natural ores and turn them into refined materials. The moon was a perfect place to build such facilities. It was out of the way of the questioning eyes of a very small but growing dissident sector of the scientific community.

Although, not really needed because of the greater society's homogeneity, these facilities had the dubious task of secretly making weapon systems of mass destruction. The largest of these moon plants would take the processed materials from other smaller satellite sites and construct finished products from them.

Moon-base Santral, named after one of the preeminent cartographers of the day, was the main finished production plant. Santral was the scientist that first mapped the surface of Oberonte correctly. Many other cartographers used flawed observational techniques including the use of older three-dimensional spectrography to map the topography of the moon. Santral theorized that the surface was made of thick powder and this was not the correct indicium to rely upon. Indeed, he was proved right when his ad-hoc scientific team using high-energy short wavelength radiography looked under the soft surface to find previous surveys were off in many areas by as much as a cargo ships length. This miss calculation of where the hard surface lay could have cost a brave crew its lives. However, luckily the central mapping agency agreed with Santrals' research and adopted his cartography and elevation theory for flight maps on the early expeditions to Oberonte.

After many arduous months of debate, the finance committee's doors were closed after it finished the state's budget for another year. Actually, the government's proceedings were never really open for public scrutiny. The real meetings took place with no publicity or awareness of the populace. The press was a lower arm of the Ministry of Information. Thus, there was never any unauthorized information filtered out to the people.

A full ten percent of the Cauldarian budget was secretly earmarked for the black box projects. Of which moon base Santral was one. Of this ten percent, the Santral project only consumed a small portion. But the impact of the research and the eventual implementation of it would be enormous.

*   *   *

The milieu was desolate. The surface albedo was quite low due to a thick powder surface comprised of solutone. Solutone was a soft purple colored stone abundant throughout the solar system. Speculation of the powders origin ranged from the collision of a great solutone meteorite to one of massive volcanic activity that released the purple substance from the depths of Oberonte. Both theories were thought to be partially right. The solutone was advantageous in some respects and dangerous in others. For the purpose of making high explosives and high-energy electro-chemical weapons the thick powder was a godsend. The material could only be used in a processed form and set off with high-energy electrical impulses. So in case of an untimely mishap or explosion in one of the manufacturing plants, the deep powdery substance would shield the surrounding areas. This was advantageous from the safety standpoint but this was not the real reason for its choice for manufacturing and location. The real motive was that it was impossible to travel on the moon by any means without being seen. There was always a dust cloud of some sort to alert the security forces of an arrival, wanted or unwanted. This moon had many secrets, but they were only to be known by the upper echelon government officials that approved their funding.

These same administrators also had a cover story just in case rumor had started its intrusive course. The Santral base and its large compliment of lasers, for the case of hearsay, was built to help protect the public of Cauldaria from stray asteroids entering the lower Cauldarian atmosphere and becoming deadly meteors.

But one of the real reasons to put a laser base on the moon was not to protect the people, but to protect the government's faith. It was tasked to destroy any asteroids or meteors that did not have a trajectory to the spiritual land. There would also be a far more heinous purpose uncovered in the near future. This purpose would help change the minds and hearts of the average Cauldarian in the years to come.

*   *   *

Orbiting Oberonte was a large production facility that was invisible from the surface of the moon and even from the largest of the telescopes on Cauldaria. The walls of the orbiting plant were made of viewing screens stretched from corner to corner. These screens projected the light or scene from the far side to the near. The image would be the one of the other side viewed from the perspective of the observer. This electronic invisibility was broken only by power outages or computer errors.

A production plant from nowhere that had the ability to build enormous space vehicles in secret was any governments dream. But dreaming was not the Ministry of States purpose. Inside the huge silent cube in space, the workers were just finishing the buildup stage of a new class of ship. The new designation was the dreadnought class. Heavily armored and gunned. She was a beast and a predator. Everyone involved in her production was sworn to secrecy. Fortunately, not everyone would abide this. The dreadnought would in the future, not only be a part of history, she would make history.

Of Green Illusions

10

The Codes

As they continued their way to the command center Michael remembered he did not retrieve the launch codes from George this morning. He used them just to irritate the launch director at the command center. He usually punched them in the launch control touch pad long before he was officially given them. The director always wondered where and how he got the code. His ship could not go anywhere without them. Unless the small code was punched in, the ship could only achieve fifty percent power. This was just enough for checking the engine performance and the onboard systems. At fifty percent power, the ship could supposedly hover and fly just above the ground, but with little control. More power was needed for full and controlled flight for an ascent to orbit.

Michael received the codes from George. He used his computing capacity for easily figuring out these mathematical algorithms. A friend at central command that owed Michael a favor told him the information they used to produce the codes. It was a very simple formula. They took the position of the largest moon at sunrise and multiplied it by the seven numbers of the days date. This was no problem for George. He could figure it out immediately.

"Guess what? I forgot to get the codes again."

"We don't need them. We'll just wait for the launch director to issue them today."

"No, I never did like those people having control over my ship." Michael indicated.

He had a problem with authority figures that dated back to his childhood. If he had to do twice the work to get the same results, he would do it if he could get around the rules and the authority they represented. But he was always careful of not drawing attention to the fact.

He decided to call George on the way and get them. He called on the mobile transmitter that James had in his transport.

"The line's busy! I bet he is calling the damn library again. He is one of their best customers. Come on George get off the line." He encouraged his electramorph friend to learn everything he could so they could have an intelligent give and take in their personal conversations, although, he did tell George to act stupid and unintelligent when conversing with others. If he did not, it would be immediately known the procedure for his logic gates were changed and the government would confiscate and destroy him.

He tried one more time. It was still busy. He knew George's schedule and it never varied unless something unusual happened. He looked at his watch and thought George should be down for regeneration now. He gave another call, just for the heck of it. The line was still busy. Now, he had an uneasy feeling in the pit of his stomach.

"Something's wrong, I feel something isn't right."

"You can say that again," replied James.

"Do you know something that I should know?"
He did not get a response.

"I know we don't really have the time, but I would like to go back and check in on him."

"You might not like what you find."

"What the hell does that mean?"

"Nothing, disregard it. I'm just running off at the mouth." James said quietly.

"Turn around, go back. I have to check on him." Michael snapped.

"I think we should get to the ship as soon as possible."

"James, he's my friend."

With that statement, James immediately turned the transport around and sped through the paths back to Michaels. He could see the worry in his friend's eyes.

"We'll be there in a short while. It's probably nothing." James said, now trying to comfort him, but James knew better. He knew what was probably waiting for Michael.

"Can't this thing go any faster, it's brand new? Push it James."

"OK, all right, I'm pushing it!" The faster they sped through the paths the longer it seemed to take.

Finally, as they pulled up to his house another transport was simultaneously leaving at high speed.

"Did you see its markings?"

"No, it was moving too fast." James replied.

Michael opened the door and was out and running even before James stopped his transport. James sat in the transport for a moment before he went in. He knew what his friend would find and wanted to give him a moment alone.

Michael burst through the door. It was easy because the lock was already broken. He entered and could not believe his eyes. His whole house was ransacked. He immediately ran to the central pod where George's unformed mass should be regenerating and processing information. The pod was empty. Where was his friend?

"George!" He yelled. He knew there would be no response, but he continued to yell it as he searched room to room. James walked in to see his always cool and collected friend in a frenzied state.

"Who did this?" Michael was looking for an answer.

"What did they do to you? My God, what did they do to you?" He questioned as he found his friend lying on the floor, disconnected from his central pod. It was the equivalent of being dead. Electramorphs were created or 'born' on their central pods. If taken away or separated from the pod it would be commensurate to a decapitation.

He knelt down picking up part of what was now a dead slippery silver substance. His friend oozed through his fingers as a lifeless blob. There was nothing left of his sentience. There were no more memories, warm moments of conversation and most of all there was the end of a friendship, which they both valued highly. There was just a silvery substance spread all over the floor.

Michael sat there barely aware of James presence, but aware enough of it for him not to cry. He wanted to cry, but he was his commanding officer.

He could not let James see him in that condition. Instead, he turned his emotions into anger.

Michael whispered to his dead companion as he lay on the floor. "Whoever did this will pay? I promise you that."

James walked over to console his friend and commander.

"Why?" Michael whispered again.

"I have a feeling you'll find out soon enough." James said with a sorrowful voice.

He pulled himself together and decided not remember his friend along with hatred of the people who did this. Hatred was a debilitating emotion and he wanted none of it. But he vowed again that he would find out who and why this was done.

They both stood from their kneeling positions and walked to the door where Michael noticed something out of the corner of his eye. Part of George's silvery substance spelled out something. He walked over to the corner were a puddle was located. It read: '3492047 with love, good friend.'

With his dying spasms, George did his last duty and gave Michael the launch codes for the day, but more importantly, he let Michael know he thought of him as a friend and loved him also.

11

The Architect

She always had a caring soul. Even from her early childhood days when other children were only concerned with toys and playing games. She had taken on the responsibility of raising her four younger brothers while her father and mother worked. Her parents always had to labor at numerous jobs to make ends meet for their family and thus were not around as much as they would have liked to be. Therefore, Verna, as the eldest sibling, took on the job of helping in the nurturing of her brothers. Even though she treasured her brothers and loved caring for them, the pressure took its toll on her young psyche. But it also and most importantly enhanced her character. This would serve her well, later in life.

These qualities became useful while designing the space station Gwanameade. She was the senior architect on the project. It was in fact her design that was selected from the design competition held by the Ministry of Science. In winning the competition, she had the responsibility of assembling a collection of builders that would eventually construct the huge space station. Verna also had to find and work with a number of less-accomplished architects to finish the drafting and designing of the final prototype of her original design. She had the grand design of her layout out in her blueprints, but needed dozens more draftsmen to finish the simpler details in her plans. White-collar contracting regulations specified that all government bid contracts use a high number of new university graduates. This rule was supposedly introduced to help young graduates get experience after their studies were over. But everyone knew the government included them because it was less expensive to employ inexperienced workers and the cost of the publicly funded projects would be reduced.

The leadership qualities she garnered from her childhood again made a difference in her professional life. The final design phase of the enormous project was scheduled to take twice the amount of time it actually did. She had chosen her team well. It was comprised of aeronautical engineers and orbital architects. The orbital architects were from a brand new area of study involving the design of pressurized habitats needed for living in space. The combination of these two fields of study was a brilliant move on her part.

The Ministry of Science was so ecstatic with the rapid progress of the design phase they threw out the plans for a public lottery to choose a name for the space platform. They gave Verna the choice. She immediately chose Gwanameade. No one knew the origin of the name; many had tried a guess and all were wrong. This only added to the mystery and speculation of the ever-popular city in the sky.

She organized a consortium of six large manufacturing corporations to construct the station in three phases. Also integrated into the fabrication process was a government group charged with erecting all of the electronics and communication arrays. This was not her choice, but a requirement of the contract. The final assembly of the communication arrays would be at the end of the third construction phase to be completed and it was the most secretive. The government did not want civilians mucking around and asking questions, so during this last stage all non-government personnel were ordered to leave the platform and back to Cauldaria.

It was during this last phase of construction when Verna first met Scott Edwards, the future commander of Gwanameade. Verna gave the opening address to the audience in the first series of introduction lectures for the operations staff. The huge auditorium was full to capacity. The atmosphere in the hall was electrifying. The room was full of professionals, but everyone was acting like children anticipating the opening of birthday gifts. It was impossible to find anyone without a beaming smile.

Scott went back stage to greet the keynote speaker and to congratulate her on the success of the design and building of Gwanameade.

Scott made his way through the mingling crowd and reached out his hand, "Hello, you must be Verna?"

"Yes, who are you?"

"Scott Edwards, It seems I will be the first commander of your creation."

"So you were the one chosen to lead the first crew. I hear you are highly qualified, but aren't you part of the military?"

"Yes, I'm on contract with the Ministry of Science for four years. My last assignment gave 'the powers that be' a good look at my experience and capabilities. I guess someone over there likes me."

"I'm glad they chose a commander with a level head on his shoulders."

He did not know if she had heard the truth about his last command, so he looked at her with a wry look on his face, trying to figure out if her comment was a compliment or a stab at his character.

She noticed the look on his face and interjected quickly, "No, I think what you did, had taken a great deal of courage. Not many people would have made the hard decisions you had to make in that situation. I admire you for what you did and thankful they picked you for the station."

He reached out his hand again in friendship, "Thank you for your words. They mean a lot coming from you."

In many ways, he reminded her of Scott, her younger brother with the same name. In the near future they would build a bond analogous to the one she had with her brothers.

*　　　*　　　*

Scott Edwards previous command assignment resulted in the unfortunate deaths of thirteen of the ninety crew members under his command. The small observation platform was a one of a kind experimental orbiting laboratory built to test the feasibility of numerous sub-systems needed for a much larger space station.

Part of his crew was testing new bulkhead technology for use in the platforms outer rings. They were strengthened sections that would have the stations positional thrusters attached to them. The new chemical rocket thrusters were installed on all the bulkhead attachment points with ease. But the crew never knew the Ministry of Science had sent the thrusters without the usual testing of the aft combustion chambers. These tests were critical and were used to assess the strength of the metal walls that contained and redirected the highly explosive fuel/oxygen mix. Someone low in the manufacturing process decided to forgo the tests to save on production expenses. The accident investigation revealed the low-level managers reasoning was since the early period of space flight these small thrusters rarely exploded. He explained there was only a one in a million probability that one would fail.

Edwards flipped the gravity induction button to the *on* position. This would ignite the positional thrusters and start the platform rotating, thus inducing gravity. They started with a large bang. The thruster attached to the experimental bulkhead outside the control room was the only one to explode.

The crew of thirteen engineers conducting the experiments in the room on the other side of the bulkhead died within minutes. They might have survived the initial explosion but the succeeding envelopment of un-pressurized space burst all of their arterial walls and they bled out of every orifice to the frozen non-oxygenated space around them. The forensics concluded it had taken up to two agonizing minutes for them to expire.

The resulting force from the explosion of the thruster sent the platform in an uncontrollable spiral, which would inevitably send it on a trajectory towards the planet and eventually burn up in the lower atmosphere. Scott immediately ordered an evacuation to Cauldaria using the escape pods installed only two days before. There were a few that thought the platform could be saved, but he was adamant about the orders he gave. He knew if one thruster blew, the others might also. Strapped in the last escape pod that left the platform he started a preprogrammed maneuver using the remaining rockets to reorient the station. It seemed to work fine for a few seconds and he thought his decision to evacuate might have been wrong. Then a second rocket exploded. This detonation pierced the stations main fuel tank and the whole platform exploded before their eyes.

The government investigation concluded that Edwards followed all procedures and saved the rest of the sixty-seven crewmembers from a similar fate as the thirteen. The investigation was not made public as the ministry members did not want to admit responsibility for the mishap. So without any official explanation of the accident everyone had assumed it was the fault of the commander. After all, he was in charge at the time and everyone thought it was his responsibility for the safety of his crew.

Most of those professionals connected to the space program knew better and were disheartened that he was not recognized for his leadership in the saving of his remaining crew. However, Scott knew he did the right thing and that was enough for him.

12

Shot In The Dark

Events were moving quite rapidly onboard Gwanameade since the day before. As usual, the previous morning started rather uneventfully. It was a regular scheduled day off for all personnel. The normal work schedule for Cauldarians included three days of work and four days of rest. But the crew and scientific staff aboard the station had a different on-off arrangement. They had a seven day on and one day off rotation. This was partially due to necessity but most of the men and women were also highly motivated and loved their professions, so the long workweeks were actually well received among the majority of the teams on the ship.

Sandy Atretea and Kay Warran were a happily married couple and the senior instructors for the orbital radar array on the station. They just ended a training session for two other radar operator crews that were comprised of two or three siblings each. Research and practical experience showed that to run the combined highly reactive infrared ocular and radar system there had to be an elevated degree of communication between the operators. It was proved that long-term married couples or siblings were usually unsurpassed at communicating or knowing what the other was about to say or do. Even better at this art were twins, but Cauldarian twins were statistically one in a million and highly sought after in other professions and their high temperamental nature often outweighed their usefulness.

The first team of trainees Jori, Jamie and Jensen were sisters and highly tuned into each other's feelings. Their empathy seemed to flow from one to the other quite effortlessly. Their interaction was incomparable, especially during the extremely stressful situations of training.

The second of the two trainee teams was comprised of a brother and sister. The elder brother Justin was a highly competitive type and the younger sister, Jessica, had the same attributes as her older brother. In some very closely aged siblings, competitiveness would manifest its self between the two and would be a very divisive trait. But Justin and Jessica learned at an early age to help each other and use their aligned qualities together and in opposition to others to excel in whatever they endeavored.

After training, these two teams would join a third journeyman group, David and Steffani, for around the clock deep space infrared mapping and close in charting of their solar system with the stations huge radar and ocular arrays.

The group was attempting to chart the whole area inside their planetary system. They were also just beginning a survey of an area at the edge of their system just discovered. It was full of elusive dark matter and a property even less understood: dark energy. The dark energy, strangely enough, did not exactly correlate with the area of dark matter. They seemed to be in the same general area but not connected, they were two different entities.

Sandy and Kay had recently made the discovery of the unknown dark energy while fine-tuning the radar and the stations huge infrared collector with the smaller x-ray module connected to it. They had the infrared device pointed towards the area just ahead of where the dark matter started. This was done so they could start at the edge and make a clean sweep through it, sector by sector. Kay had inadvertently left the x-ray module connected to infrared unit. They were using it the day before for energy studies concerning the three neighboring galaxies and all of their associated energy-rich black holes.

When Sandy had aligned the infrared system and flipped the power switch, the x-ray receiver started to howl its electronic song of discovery. At first he couldn't believe it. Energy in an area of space where there were no celestial bodies or any possible reason for it. Its location was close to the area of dark matter, but these areas were different, they were devoid of everything, life, energy, even light.

*   *   *

Early in the morning on their one-day off, Sandy and Kay were leisurely eating breakfast and dividing the work schedule for the observations of the dark energy region. They were discussing whether to put their journeyman crew on the next shift or to use one of the two very capable trainee crews when it happened.

Sandy always wore boots and had them propped up on the table as he sat back in his chair. He leaned his head back opened his mouth extra wide to take a man sized bite of his breakfast roll. He was acting silly and knew Kay would get a little peeved at him, but deep down and by the look she gave him, he knew she loved and cherished his silliness.

He was just about to bite a big piece off with a big smile on his face when it hit. The first one smashed through the large radar dish outside. The percussion wave knocked Sandy cleanly off his chair. Kay screamed as he hit the floor. She ran to him and then the second one hit. It smashed into the computer room next to the control station where Sandy and Kay were. The whole area shook violently with the two impacts. Both the dish and the computer room were demolished.

"What the hell was that?" Sandy yelled.

Screaming at the top of her voice, "I don't know!"

He looked to the radar console as Kay helped him up to his feet. "Look Kay, It was a meteor strike. It came in at such an oblique angle our proximity sensors never picked it up."

She stared at the screen for a few seconds and looked over to Sandy, "I've never seen any meteors come in from that direction before. I hope it was just an anomaly."

"I hope so, too." Sandy replied.

It was a scheduled day off so there were only a few emergency personnel on duty at the time and they were located on the other side of the outermost ring of the station. It would take them a while to get to the area of the first and second hits.

Luckily, the integrity of their room was intact, but Kay looked through the clear wall of the computer room. The outer wall was obliterated. The room was open to the vacuum of space. She told Sandy, "Go to the dock excursion room and bring back two space suits."

"Why?"

"Look into the computer room."

In the darkness there was a strange glow coming from the far corner. They both knew their lives were about to change.

There were three other known strikes on the outer rings of Gwanameade. But they impacted and went straight through the other side for an eventual fall to Cauldaria. Only one meteorite survived.

13

Ascent

Michael and James arrived at the ground station and it looked deserted. They both knew the current series of meteor showers made ascents to the geostationary platform extremely hazardous. The numerous onboard computers and instruments could not be trusted because of the electrostatic disturbances the meteors induced in the atmosphere, so they were both a little on edge. The only crew competent or maybe stupid enough to try was Michaels.

As Michael entered the station first, he noticed a different feeling in the air. He could not quite put his finger on it, but something was not right. No one was in sight. All the equipment was running and operational. The station could and quite often did run in an automated state. But he had a strange feeling. As if someone was watching every movement he was making. Just as he was about to call out and say *OK* the jokes over, the communications panel came alive. A small holographic image of the commander of Gwanameade, the Cauldarians largest space platform, rested in the air above the communications console.

It was an old and welcomed friend, Scott Edwards. He was someone with whom he could talk about anything no matter how personal. But he felt somehow today's communication from him was different. His opening line was terse and to the point. He also sounded very official and tense; these were very strange and unusual actions coming from his friend.

Michael thought, *now I know something is wrong, I had better take his queue and keep our conversation short and to the point. I'll wait to talk to him in person when I get to Gwanameade.*

"Good morning Captain Norton; your orders are to start your ascent in no more than four hours. You will make the flight with only your co-pilot onboard, this means the rest of your crew will be grounded by orders of the Ministry of State."

Commander Edwards knew as well as Michael that the Ministry of State had no authority to ground his crew. Michael decided to play along in this circumstance.

"OK, commander. The Vernacaria will be up in approximately three hours," Michael said with a slight and confused smile.

They both left the control center and headed to launch pad number four where Michael's ship was located.

As they walked to the launch pad they turned their heads and looked at each other as if they knew this was not going to be a normal flight. James then asked Michael a question that he already knew the answer to. "Why did you really get into the flying business? Why didn't you become a teacher, farmer or something else, something safe?"

He stopped dead in his tracks and gave James a puzzled look. "With everything that has happened today that is one off the wall question, why do you ask?"

"Well, sometimes when you fly, it seems you want to risk it all and when you're not flying you play it safe. I know you like the freedom you get from flight. Wouldn't you also like that same degree of freedom in your nonprofessional life. And how much would you risk getting it?"

"What the hell are you talking about? Are you questioning my flying technique or my character?"

"No, you are my best friend and someday you might find out something about me, and I wonder how you will take it. I wonder if you will truly understand."

Michael shook his head and started walking toward the ship again. James started a few steps behind him and hopped along to catch up.

"You say sometimes I risk it all and other times I play it safe. Let me answer your question in this way. I guess that I do risk a lot in my profession—I'm happy go lucky. I'm very confident in my skills. But when it comes to my personal life I play it safe as I can, because I feel a lesser control. I still have vivid memories of the Unification School we were sent to."

His friend instantly responded, "What if your personal and your professional lives mix? How would you handle it?"

"I've never had that happen yet, have you?" Michael retorted.

"Yes, I'll tell you about it someday."

Michael gazed at him, "What the hell, you sure are cryptic today. I feel almost every answer you give me lately hides something."

Without looking at his friend, James replied, "I think you'll know soon enough."

Michael shook his head and his hands at the same time indicating that he was tired of the conversation and wanted to end it.

*　　　　　*　　　　　*

They were both still a little bit in awe of their ship and it could be seen in their eyes as they approached her. James started the preflight walk around on the craft as soon as he arrived under her engines. Although he was still upset about the events at his house last night and what happened to George this morning, he thought he could still do a good job and he knew he had to make the trip to Gwanameade at least one more time.

He decided to do an in-depth check because of the crew-less ascent that was ordered by the Ministry. This is when Michael appreciated having James as his copilot because he had a knack at finding the little things that everyone else would miss. He intended to inspect the ships new quantum drives thoroughly this morning. The new quantum technologies still had James a little worried as they had so much more power than the old chemical power plants that he was used to operating.

These new engines used the same power that fueled the stars in the heavens. The quantum theory sets forth that the smallest of all particles that can be thought of are not stable and uniform, but are unsteady and violent. They are theorized to look like small strings of pure vibrating energy. These small particles are continually releasing their power, or the equivalent to infinitesimally small detonations and then reabsorbing that same force, and ejecting it out again, and so on until time itself would stop. This unlimited fuel would eventually give the Cauldarians the freedom to traverse the universe. Their engines could accelerate unerringly forever, since they would no longer have the need to feed off internal fuel. The only operational limit to velocity would ironically be that which the early airfoil based aircraft had to cope with. Specifically the heat and pressure caused by the friction of the craft with its surrounding environment.

The Cauldarian scientists had incorporated another new technology to overcome the problem of friction by the matter of space. This matter in the form ionic particles was sparse in the vacuum of space, but at the acceleration of one-third the speed of light even a sub-atomic particle would rip the ship apart like a bullet hitting a thin sheet of tin foil.

The scientists devised a new and yet unproved technique of pushing an electromagnetic field with encapsulated ice particles in front of the bow of the ship. The electromagnetic field served as a permeable envelope that kept the large ice particles in and let the small ion particles through. Once the ion particles hit the ice they would be absorbed by the cold mass or deflected to the side, out of the field of travel of the ship. The ice was replaceable through the osmosis of pure hydrogen, which was abundantly available throughout the universe. Thus, a permanent shield for the sub-light speed spacecraft was at hand for the crew to overcome the friction of deep space high-speed journeys.

These new technologies would most likely help change the Cauldarians knowledge base and their way of thinking as the government reluctantly looked toward the stars. Knowledge and understanding were entities that no one or thing could hold back as long as a people or even one Cauldarian could still dream.

*   *   *

Michael knew his ship would pass the preflight with little or no problem as it usually did. James with his usual thoroughness did find a few irregularities in the communication equipment setup, but these were within acceptable limits. The communication stacks were new units given to all shuttles by the Ministry of State. Michael thought it was very suspicious for the Ministry to foot the bill, but he decided to take the new equipment and accept the Ministry's benign explanation of its generosity. He had a feeling he would regret this decision at a later date, and he would.

James and Michael entered the ship through the crew entryway. This large pressure door could fit ten Cauldarians in the entry port. It was easier to fit through than the small pilot door next to the cockpit, which had to be accessed by way of a three-story elevator. They used the ships small internal lift to gain access to the upper flight crew level. They both entered the cockpit, which was spacious by any standard. James strapped into his flight seat first and Michael second.

They both scanned the myriad of instruments that occupied the panels in front of them. Michael felt at home here. This was one of the finest ships that Cauldaria had. She was fast and full of grace. The agility of the ship still amazed everyone that saw her fly, although, much of this finesse could only be accounted for by the piloting skills of its Captain.

Her official name was Cauld 3521, but everyone knew her by the name Vernacaria. This name belonged to a beautiful blue star cluster that was one of the many objects in the night sky that Michael watched and dreamed about as a child. But the real meaning of the name no one knew except Michaels close friends. It was a derivative of the name of the love of his life. It amused him to think that he dreamed of a blue star cluster as a child and now as an adult he dreamed of a woman, both with similar names. She was the designer of the space station Gwanameade. He would never forget their first meeting...

*   *   *

Michael was amazed at the complexity of the new space station. He never thought it possible to build something this enormous in the vacuum of space. He walked around the stations corridors all morning long with an irrecoverable smile on his face. He was like a child that was discovering for the first time a new and beautiful corner of the universe that was all his own. The walls of the corridors and non-living areas were completely transparent. The new clear polysamtrite material had certainly lived up to its manufactures claims to be the clearest solid material known to Cauldaria. The view was spectacular; walking through the corridors was like walking in space with the stars all encompassing. Michael thought the designer to be a genius. He started to walk to the planetarium dome to hear an informal speech to be given by her.

On the way, he stopped to watch a shuttle disembark from the station. It was at a ships length away from the station and its old chemical engines spewed forth a beautiful plume of golden sparkles. The sparkles hit against the transparent walls of the corridor and flew around it like fireflies against the starry night. Michael thought it could not get more beautiful than this, and then it did.

She had walked between him and the scene outside. She turned, stopped and looked his way. The golden sparkles looked as if they were caressing the outline of her body; they shimmered and danced about her. Michael then looked into her eyes. He would never be the same again…

The light reflected from her warm blue eyes across the corridor to his. Her soft image went through his eyes and down to his very soul. Michael's heart felt as if it had stopped, he sensed as if he was in another dimension. His movements seemed to slow down quite measurably. He could not take his eyes from hers. Nothing else in the universe mattered at this moment. He had been with other beautiful women before, but this was something more, he had an all-enveloping feeling that he needed to be with her always. Michael had to say something before she left the corridor. All he could muster to speak out was a silly little murmur. His blood then ran hot and his face filled with the warmth, it was a full-blown blush. He had made a fool of himself, he thought.

She returned his blundered communication attempt with a warm and understanding smile.

Michael was in love. He knew that he would always desire her for as long as he would live. Michael's life had changed, all from one glance.

*   *   *

James and Michael finished the exterior and interior preflight an hour before the expected take off time. Michael had already decided to take off as early as possible, due to the strange demeanor of Commander Edwards's holographic message. He also yearned to hold Verna in his arms again, to feel her touch and to look into her loving eyes once more.

They started the onboard communications equipment of the Vernacaria, to contact the orbiting space station, independent of the ground control facility. Michael flipped the master switch and nothing happened.

He looked at James and asked, "Didn't you check the com equipment stack?"

James looked back at him in amazement and answered, "Of course I did, it was one of the first things on the cockpit preflight checklist."

He looked again at the communications panel and recycled a few switches.

"Nothing..."

He knew the new equipment from the Ministry of State would go tits up just when he needed it most. They both gave the com panel a few whacks to jostle and hopefully revive the dead equipment. James even started talking to it, as if the inanimate object would suddenly come to life and say, "Sorry guy's, just resting." They looked at each other in disgust and just as Michael was about to abort the flight a light buzzing sound turned his attention away from the com panel. The sound was coming from a small multi-frequency two-way transceiver that he bought and possessed illegally.

The State did not tolerate any uncensored communications between the Cauldarian people.

Michael used it only for the express purpose to communicate with Verna or Scott onboard Gwanameade, uncensored of course. He turned the small unit on and received only one message that was repeated over and over:

"Michael, we need your help now, we have a--" Scott's voice echoed.

His transmission was broken off in the middle of the hurried message. He tried to call him back, but to no avail, his transceiver was not responding. The communications panel in the Vernacaria then suddenly lit up. The Ministry was now transmitting new orders to the shuttle.

Michael yelled, "I knew it, the Ministry has control of our communications equipment. I should have never agreed to have it installed."

James copied the orders on his flight log and handed them to Michael. The new instructions indicated they were not to take off due to new and very significant developments in the security of Gwanameade.

Just as he finished reading the last word of the message, Michael looked at James and smiled while reaching for the ignition switch. He pushed it in and said, "Screw the Ministry!" The ascent was on.

14

So That They Might See

After entering the launch code into the flight computer, the engines of the Vernacaria started with a slow whine and a little vibration. The noise and vibration were caused by the initial start up revolutions of the great air turbine fans that were used to begin the ascent of the huge ship. The fans were encased in tubular housings for directional flow of the turbine compressed air. These tubular housings were mounted on gimbals for multi-azimuth steering. The large fans were used for creating positive air pressure to propel the craft through the dense lower atmosphere of Cauldaria. The housings also had attached on them small chemical burning thrusters for minute maneuvers in the so-called vacuum of space.

The openings on the back end of the fan housings opened and closed with louver like panels. When these were closed, the air was redirected from the back to small openings on the inner side of the fan housings and through the directional gimbals. This ducted air then went into the ships main empennage and ultimately into the quantum drives.

These new drives had no moving parts. This fact pleased Michael because this meant there was nothing to break down on the proposed long distance voyages through space.

The vibration of the engines smoothed out with the increasing revolutions of the turbine fans. Michael tested the full directional stability of his ship when the fans were at seventy five percent of maximum thrust. Everything seemed to be working as advertised. Michael then pushed the throttles full forward to the throttle stops. The turbines were now producing power at one hundred fifty percent of normal. Just as the turbine RPM indicator passed the red line Michael released the locking clamps that held his ship to the ground.

The Vernacaria lifted off smoothly and swiftly as if she had never belonged on the surface at all. The ship was extremely responsive to even the smallest control inputs by the flight crew.

Michael then rotated the ship along its vertical axis one hundred eighty degrees to get a view of the command center as he gained height.

After the turn, James could now see a tram approaching the take off pad at high speed. It had markings on the side indicating it was one of the Cauldarian cabinet member's trams.

All of the ships communications equipment suddenly came on-line again and bristled with life. Michael now knew for sure the Ministry had control of his com stack. There were repeated messages from the Ministry for the Vernacaria to stand down. Michael then also noticed the tram.

"Who's that coming up on the launch pad?" Michael yelled.

James sarcastically replied, "After that wild party at my house last night I can't really see or hear anything this morning."

Michael returned his comment with only a smile. They were on the way to Gwanameade--with a little help from the Ministries new quantum drives.

Michael laughed at the irony, because the Vernacaria was one of the first ships to have quantum drives installed in it. The Office of Science, a sub-cabinet of the Ministry of State was the department that pushed for the new drives. Their reasoning for the new engines was quite innocent. They wanted to save on the fuel consumption of the shuttles as the private shuttle fleet was growing and thus diminishing the Cauldarian energy resources considerably. What they did not account for was the universe was now wide open for exploration. They were now able to go beyond the local area of Cauldarian space. The Ministry of State was about to lose its tight grip on the people of Cauldaria.

As it is in most scientific endeavors that are successful, the knowledge that is gained tends to influence the society in which it serves. This was not the intent of the Ministries sub-department, but Michael knew this is what would eventually happen. He knew his people would, in the future, start to ask questions on the makeup of the universe they were about to traverse and follow their own hearts and explore their own convictions as he did as a child, before the State straitened him out and pointed him down their correct path.

He knew the Ministry would eventually lose its battle for the minds and hearts of the Cauldarian people. He wondered how long this would take. How many generations it would take for change? The Vernacaria and Gwanameade were to be the first stepping-stones to their people's enlightenment.

James turned the volume up on the communication equipment and he looked at Michael with a confused look.

"Is that Minister Hauldan?" James asked.

"Yeah, that's him all right."

"What in the hell is he doing here, so close to the pad?"

"I don't know, nor do I care." Michael said with a sarcastic tone.

Steve Hauldan was the current Minister of State. He held one of the most powerful positions in the Cauldarian government. He was well known as a ruthless politician. He also had a strong power base among the elite in Cauldarian society.

Michael thought him to be a closed minded, vein, little man. He had met the Minister a couple times during the building process of the Vernacaria and lost respect for him on a later occasion when he had the misfortune of taking the Ministry cabinet members aloft for a short ceremonial flight.

Michael thought of the flight, and this is why he held Steve Hauldan in such disdain.

*   *   *

It was the first regular flight of the Vernacaria, after her successful flight test program. This first flight was set-aside for the top government officials, to dazzle them, as the minister had put it. Hauldan led the other cabinet members around the launch pad like he owned it. In a sense, while functioning as the Minister of State, he did. She was a privately owned ship, but the ministries regulations and numerous conditions effectively made it a quasi-private state venture.

He then led the group of governmental luminaries into the Vernacaria to take their respective seats that were bolted down in the bottom most cargo level of the ship. The ship was not fully fitted out yet. The crew seating area just below the cockpit level was not scheduled to get its seats installed for another few days. But the Minister insisted on the early flight, so he could show off the fleet's newest vessel. The timing of this publicity stop was perfect for Hauldan's re-election campaign tour, but the ships amenities were not ready for passengers yet, as Michael would prove to him after takeoff.

Michael asked Hauldan, "Minister, as I said in my earlier communiqué, the ship is not--"

Hauldan cut him off in mid sentence, "Captain Norton, this is the finest space shuttle on Cauldaria. I know of your concerns, but she passed all of the flight tests with flying colors, pardon the pun."

"Yes but--"

"Captain take this ship up or I'll find someone who will."

Michael shrugged his shoulders and said, "OK, you're the boss."

He told all the cabinet members and the Minister to strap in tight, as they would be experiencing zero and negative G's during portions of the flight. That meant there would be a tendency for everything not strapped down to float about the cargo bay.

Michael noticed that Hauldan strapped into a row of seats that were off by themselves, in front of the other rows where the lowly sub-cabinet members sat. Hauldan must have thought he was better than the rest so he sat in front by himself.

Michael did not have the heart to tell the Minister that the row of seats he was sitting on was not bolted to the floor like the others.

He powered up the engines to one hundred percent and released the locking clamps that held the Vernacaria to the ground. He let her accelerate to the escape velocity speed that objects needed to break the gravitational bonds of Cauldaria and to achieve orbit. The hull of the ship and everything contained in it now had the weight of ten positive G's against it. This meant an average Cauldarian would be forced down in their chair with ten times the force of gravity they would have in normal and level flight or standing on the ground. The Minister and the cabinet members were now being squashed in their seats by the invisible force. They now weighed ten times their normal weights.

Just before attaining orbit Michael slapped the control stick sideways and in a heartbeat, the Vernacaria was past the vertical. At a negative one hundred thirty five degrees, Michael pulled the throttles back to Idle. The ship was now heading back to the ground and in a zero gravitational state. The Minister was now floating.

After a few more disorientating maneuvers Michael decided to land and see how his know-it-all passenger had faired. He used the convenient inside crew lift to descend to the cargo bay where the passengers were seated. By the time Michael entered the cargo bay all the cabinet members had exited the ship. Only Hauldan was left, sitting on the floor and shaking.

Michael had the good sense not to laugh. He then noticed the Minister, the most powerful person on Cauldaria, had wet his pants. Michael's humorous outlook on the situation changed to one of pity. This was probably the first time in Hauldan's adult life when he did not have complete control over the situation, over a crazy man in the cockpit!

Thinking about this poor man shaking and sitting on the floor in his own urine disturbed him. But then he thought about how the Minister acted before the flight and a big grin appeared on his face.

*   *   *

James also remembered the first flight with Hauldan, looked over at Michael, and knew what he was thinking. He had no love for the Minister either. Hauldan was now directly below them on the launch pad and still transmitting the message for the Vernacaria to stand down.

"James, he actually wants us to stand down."

"No way, if you throttle back now, you'll crush him underneath the ship."

"Oh well, it was just an idea; besides nothing is going to keep me away from Verna today." Michael said as he thought of the broken message from commander Edwards that was transmitted earlier. Both his friend and his lover were in trouble onboard Gwanameade station, he and his co-pilot were on their way to help.

Michael thought of Verna during the ascent. She was in his thoughts most of the time--all the time, actually. He saw her when he closed his eyes, when he looked off into the distance, when he paused from what he was doing to take a deep breath. He remembered how, in the moonlight, her soft blue eyes glittered back speckles of beautiful azure light... The cute little crinkle on the side of her nose when she laughed... How her delicate touch felt as she lovingly caressed him... Her tantalizing voice when she would sigh and mellifluously whisper, "I love you."

Of Green Illusions

15

Dreadnought

The Vernacaria was ascending to orbit at its usual speed. It would take only a few minutes to escape the tight grip of gravity at regular velocity, but all afternoon to orbit Cauldaria. The Ministries rules of orbital space transit indicated slow velocities. These rules were a holdover from the early days of orbital travel, when shuttle engines were highly unreliable. They had a tendency of blowing up at high throttle positions in zero gravity. The Vernacaria's engines were of a new design and the crew dreaded using the old velocity rules. So Michael decided to utilize the new quantum drives to arrive at Gwanameade before the scheduled docking time. He knew this would surprise a few people and anger one — Hauldan.

"I'm going to punch in the quantum drives," Michael told James, "hold on."

"Hold on to what?"

James grabbed the ejection seat handles and then laughed, "Damn, you sure do scare me sometimes."

"Hey, you're scaring me. Don't pull hard on those handles; if you do, you're out of here."

"Don't worry I'm holding on with a light touch," He said with a big smile, "it seems whenever I fly with you my hands are always close to the ejection seat handles. I think I'll caress these beautiful cold metal handles until your done playing space ranger with the new engines." Although, he did use his left hand to switch on the magnetic gravity suits they wore.

Michael instilled great confidence in his copilot when he grabbed the lever that controlled the thrust of the quantum drives and then let out a boyish sound, "Vroom, Vroom."

James took his hand off the right handle and smacked his head with it, rolled his eyes and said, "You're insane, what have I let myself in for?"

Michael replied, "The ride of your life."

The quantum engines were not engineered to work where they were now, in the dense atmosphere of Cauldaria. No one with a level head had ever tried or even thought about the idea of trying to engage the powerful drives in the lower Cauldosphere, except Michael. The large hydrogen content would most likely make the drives go to critical mass in just a few seconds. In addition, the friction from the fast moving air around the hull would probably melt the ship as the ice deflection system could only be used in the sparse molecular vacuum of space. Not all these facts would stop Michael for a second.

"Are you really going to do this?"

"Damned right," he answered.

He pushed the quantum throttles one quarter forward and then did something that baffled James. He reversed the thrust of the lift off turbine fans so the thrust was pointed forward of the ships direction of travel. This would create a barrier heat shield of cool air and would prevent the hull from melting from the oncoming friction. Once he had the air shield established he pushed the quantum throttles full forward for a few seconds, just enough to get the engines up to speed and transverse the escape velocity needed to get the Vernacaria to orbit.

"James, read off the quantum gas temperature and power production off the gauges in percentages, while I fly her."

"Forty percent power."

"Fifty percent power."

"Michael, we're already redlining on the gas temperature. She's going to go critical!"

"I'm going to throttle back," James insisted.

"Take your hand off the throttle and learn something," Michael snapped back.

Michael then used some of the super cooled liquid hydrogen left on board from the old chemical engines. He flipped a switch and vented the super cooled mixture overboard and into the slipstream of the ship. The hydrogen collectors at the tail end of the ship caught the subfreezing compound and ingested it into the quantum drive system.

"Gas temperatures are dropping to normal parameters," James indicated, while he wiped the sweat from his brow.

"Sixty percent power."

"Seventy percent power."

"Eighty percent power."

Michael pulled the throttles back slightly, "Don't want to press my luck."

The Vernacaria was now streaking through the morning sky. From the ground she looked as if there were a rainbow following from behind her. She was traveling so fast that someone on the ground would only see her hydrogen exhaust rainbow for a few fleeting seconds and then she would be out of sight.

They were achieving an optimal orbital track and Michael pulled the quantum throttles full back.

The engines silenced with just a small shudder. He simultaneously shut the turbines down.

The Vernacaria attained a high parabolic trajectory. She was hurdling through space towards Gwanameade with all engines off. She approached the space station at high speed, but all that was needed to slow her down would be a deft hand and the small maneuvering thrusters that were installed to help her negotiate intricate movements in space.

Michael maneuvered his ship in close to the outer docking ring of Gwanameade and did something he usually hated to do, but in this instance, he was just plain tired from all the day's events. He turned the auto-docking sequencer on. This device would take him out of the loop and he would just sit back and watch the computers dock the ship for him.

When the Vernacaria and Gwanameade had safely coupled, James turned and asked, "Where did you learn how to do that?"

"Do what?"

"Use the quantum engines in combination with the turbines, to create a heat shield in the lower atmosphere without blowing up?"

"Nowhere..."

"What do you mean nowhere?"

"I just thought it up as I went on. I flew her by the seat of my pants."

"Well Captain," James said sarcastically, "you flew her by the seat of your pants and I think I just shit mine."

"I thought I smelled something."

The airlock doors opened and Scott Edwards stood there. "It's good to see you, Michael." He returned his greeting with a hug.

"What is going on up here? I think I've broken every rule in the book getting to the station."

"The Ministry of State has taken control over the majority of our operational systems here on Gwanameade."

"Scott, you know they can't do that."

"Well they did and they have troops on board to enforce it."

A cold shiver went down his spine, "Where's Verna?"

"She is safe for now. We have the Ministry believing that she's doing the required engineering checks on the station."

"Why has the Ministry taken over the station?"

There was a short pause before Edwards replied, "I don't know, but they boarded only one day after we had taken damage from one of the meteor showers."

"I thought Gwanameade was well out of the normal path of the showers."

"I thought so too!"

He then immediately asked, "Were there any meteorite fragments found at the impact sights?"

Scott looked away and quietly replied, "Not that I know of. There were a few shuttles docked at the time; they might know something."

He looked at his eyes and felt there was something more that he was not telling him. Then he remembered that James had made an unscheduled flight to Gwanameade the day before and wondered if that is why his home was broken into last night. Michael now knew there was something else going on and he was risking the safety of his ship by staying here, but he did not care. He wanted to do all he could to help his friends.

"Is there anything I can do to help?" Michael asked.

"We may need the Vernacaria to transport some of the personnel off the station if things heat up." Scott said.

"What do you mean, if things heat up?"

"A few of my command personnel have just sabotaged the personal communications equipment onboard the station so the Ministries troops cannot communicate with Cauldaria, we are the only ones that can use it. Although, the large telecommunication relay array for ground-to-ground transfers is still functional, the individual troops cannot transmit down, but they can still receive. They are blaming me for the failure and I'm supposed to be under house arrest."

"Then we should get you back to your quarters."

"Don't worry; I know this station better than anyone, except Verna. They don't even know you're docked here; this part of the station isn't viewable from the hub where the troops are located. The systems superstructure will hopefully block their view. But I will give you a set of false identity cards just in case you come across any of them."

"Scott, my ship and I are yours for any purpose."

He responded with a solid forearm handshake and said, "Thank you, Michael."

"We should go to the command center and see if anyone knows where Verna is."

On the far side of Cauldaria, the Archimedes was well on its way on a two-day journey to its destination of Gwanameade. The Archimedes was a huge military orbiter that was heavily armored and had incredible weapons of destruction onboard. She was extremely slow due to the mass of all the armor that the Ministry said was needed to avoid destruction by the occasional stray meteor shower. Most Cauldarians never knew she even existed. In a short while, she would make herself known to the world.

16

Reunion

After meeting with his friend, commander Edwards, Michael started the search for his love, Verna. He was told by some of the command personnel in the operations office that she was in the center station area testing the main loading dock air locks for their safe operation.

Michael started the journey from the operations center that was located on the outer hub to the central area of the station, where all of the other hubs were also connected. Each of the many linking hubs of the station had its own small loading dock with an air lock safety system installed.

He figured it wouldn't take him long to get to the main air locks and to her, because he had taken an intense interest in the stations schematics not only for the reason that he was fascinated with its structure, but he also wanted to understand and support the work that Verna had spent her life developing. He studied the stations blue prints very carefully; he knew all the short cuts. At this point, every moment felt like an eternity. His mind would race with thoughts of her. He could hardly wait. He was walking down one of the transparent corridors of the outer hub when he saw James again.

"Hey James, wait there a second."

"What's up," James said as he turned and waited for him.

"I'm looking for Verna. They told me she was in the main dock area."

"I heard she was in the outer hub dock. They were having problems there this morning."

"That's just up ahead."

"You should check there first, before wasting your time going all the way to the main dock."

"Think I'll do that, thanks James."

Michael walked up to the next intersecting corridor and over to the dock air lock system. The air lock systems had four non-transparent rooms each that had to be entered one by one to get to the dock area that was open to the vacuum of space. The first room was called the exit check station. This is where the stations personnel would shed their clothes and clean their bodies in an ionizing shower. The showers were gentle to their bodies, but it would instantly kill any bacteria living on the skin. The ion shower was to preserve the cleanliness of the space suits that they would put on in the second room. The third and fourth rooms were simply compression and decompression rooms.

Michael opened the door and peeked in. He saw her bending over, taking off her clothes for the ion shower. He quietly walked in and then slammed the door behind him to surprise her.

"Who in the..."

She never finished her sentence; she stood there half-naked with a shocked look on her face. Her expression instantly turned to a smile when she saw it was her lover. He smiled back and locked the door behind him.

Michael walked slowly toward her as he savored her look. He pulled her in close and just as she began to say, "When did you--"

He kissed her and he kissed her passionately. He hugged her so tightly she could barely breathe;

she did not mind, she felt safe and secure, but most importantly loved. They stood there hugging and kissing, time and the outside world were to be abandoned, and the only thing that mattered was their love for each other.

Michael quietly asked between their soft kisses, "Why are you checking the air lock system?"

"We've had a few unexplained failures in other air lock systems on the station in the last few days."

"Could you use some help?"

"Sure," she said, "but you'll have to take an ion shower with me if you want to use a space suit."

Michael also started to take off his clothes as she stood there watching with a growing grin. They both entered the ion shower together, holding hands as if they were newfound lovers. They always held hands or were arm in arm when they were together. This open affection seemed to make some people uneasy. Neither of them seemed to notice or care. If they did perceive any disapproval of their sincere and unguarded love for each other they would just bring their bodies closer together, an act of social defiance and one of love.

They closed their eyes, because the ion shower would temporarily blind anyone that looked at the ionizer transmitter. As the ionizer started, he let out little cries, "Help me! Help me!"

Imitating what he thought the little microorganisms on his skin would probably be saying if they could speak. Verna just held on to him tightly with her head against his chest, listened to him, and laughed. Michael could always make her smile and laugh by acting silly.

They were still disrobed while waiting for the heavy sealed door to open so they could leave the first exit check-station room on the hub of the ship. The next room held the environmental suits they would need to leave the confines of Gwanameade and enter the harsh surroundings of space.

Verna turned toward the door and started for it. Michael reached out for her hand and gently caught it. She stopped in mid stride and turned back to look at him. Verna looked into his eyes as if she was looking for the first time. Not a word was spoken. She could tell what was in his heart, what he was feeling; she knew they would be making love within minutes.

Michael gathered her into his arms and smiled. He held her close and tight. Acutely aware of the warmth and pressure of his body against hers, she gave him a fierce hug and whispered, "I want to feel your heart and warmth in me."

Michael then looked lovingly into her eyes. "I love you," he quietly whispered, and kissed her.

While kissing her deeply, his hand massaged the small of her back and she felt her knees get weak. She took a deep breath to steady herself, and then decided to abandon all caution and take the advice that her heart was giving her, she followed her weakened knees to the cushioned floor where she and Michael would be one.

A shaft of sunlight streamed through the window and fell squarely across them where they lay on the floor. Michael thought the sunlight unhindered by the Cauldarian atmosphere to be magical. He gently turned her so their heads were in the sun. The soft glimmer of light from the window played with the strands of her blonde hair and the sun flecked them with gold.

They would lie, entwined in love, all morning long...

*   *   *

They eventually suited up to exit the station and check the seals on the air locks. The space suits were made of a new material that was light and extremely strong. It had sixteen thin layers, which hugged the body tightly. Each layer had a different purpose. The inner layers were permeable and served to regulate the temperature of the body using the interaction of the suits fibers and the sweat from the body. If the body were to sweat it would expand the intertwined fibers outwardly and the area between the junctions of these expanded fibers would increase. This increase in the space in-between the fibers would allow the cold from space that filtered through the outer layers of the suit to cool the air that rested there. Conversely, if the body had a low temperature there would be less induced humidity in the fibers and they would get tighter, not letting in any cold air from the outer layers, but conserving the heat of the body. The outer layers of the suits were impermeable to everything but the small amounts of temperature variability that was needed for the function of the inner layers.

The suits had no helmets to speak of. Since the head did little moving and no physical work or have any contact with other objects. The Cauldarian engineers designed a helmet with no hard encasing features of previous designs. The small environment around the head was easily contained in an inert plasma field. This plasma field was circular in shape and emanated from a control magnet, which was incorporated in the collar of the body suit. The plasma was a normal mixture of the breathable gases that the Cauldarians inhaled on the surface of their world. The air that was used in the space suits only had one difference. The variable magnet in the neck of the suit electrically excited its molecular structure. Once the plasma was excited, it had a positive attraction to area above the magnet. The variability of the magnet created a circular disturbance that was only a few molecules thick but enough to make a gaseous shell able to contain the breathable plasma and to keep out the vacuum of space. At the back of the neck, one would wear a re-breather that would filter the used air, clean it and re-circulate it to the plasma mixture.

Michael never did feel very comfortable wearing the new suits with no hard encasing helmet for security. The two entered the last of the four rooms in the air lock system. This last room is where the decompression would take place and the area that encompassed them would be at the same pressure as the space outside of the station.

Verna started the decompression sequence, in a few moments the large outer door would open, and they would be exposed to space.

"How long will this take?" Michael asked.

"It will only be a few moments."

Michael could hear and feel the plasma field around his head start to power up.

"Hate these damn things," he whispered to himself.

Verna overheard and smiled. She patted and then held his hand to comfort and calm him.

Michael was used to piloting great ships through the hostile environments of space, not wearing a fragile little suit in it. She squeezed his hand and gave him an understanding look. She understood his anxiety and was compassionate.

Michael then decided to suck it up and act like the captain he was. He figured if anything happened that at least he was with the woman he loved.

He started to laugh, "I'm acting like an idiot, aren't I?"

"Yeah, but your my idiot."

They both sat there laughing as the outer door opened.

She instantly knew when she saw it. The hard rubber seals around the doors had been reheated and were now soft. These would eventually fail, maybe not today, maybe not tomorrow, but they would fail soon. This was just like the other air lock systems that had failed recently on the station. Something or someone was trying to cause a catastrophic failure to the integrity of the structure of Gwanameade. But why she thought? James and Scott knew.

Of Green Illusions

17

To Awaken A Sleeping Giant

When Michael and Verna had checked on a few more air locks they decided to call a meeting of all the personnel on Gwanameade they thought they could trust. They made their way to Scott Edwards' quarters to arrange the meeting. He knocked on the door. There was no answer at first, and then a second knock received a "Who is it?" from Scott.

"It's the boogie man and I've come for you."

The door opened up just a crack. James, Scott and his old mentor Charlie Dunham were standing behind it, all checking to see if it was really Michael.

Scott let them into his room, which was filled with people that he had seen around the station and known casually.

"What's going on?"

"Michael, it seems we have been beaten to the punch on calling a meeting." Verna said.

"Yeah," he blurted in amazement.

James looked around the room and found Scott's eyes. He nodded and then James turned back to Michael and asked him to sit down. He then asked if he remembered his childhood and of the religious rehabilitation school were they had first met.

"Yes, I do, I will never forget what they did to us there."

James looked around the room again, there must have been forty or so people sitting or standing around watching.

"I have never brought up that time or discussed that period of our lives during our ongoing friendship have I?"

"No, I also thought it would bring back bad memories if I spoke of it and assumed you felt the same way." Michael exclaimed.

James nodded his head to confirm what Michael had said.

"How do you feel now, about the school and our government for sending you there?"

Michael looked around the room and asked, "Can I trust these people?"

"I do, with my life." James replied.

Michael then answered, "I had hate in my heart for anything and everything involved or associated with the government for years and then I began a journey down a different path, one without hate, to explore my personal faith quietly, on my own. The anger and hate acted like toxins attacking my soul. I knew that I had to forgive to move on, intellectually and emotionally. At nights, when I was a young man, I would lie in bed and wonder how I could help free my fellow Cauldarians so they could live and believe differently from the state religion as I did. I dreamed of a world where I could openly discuss and share my version of faith with others whom had different but equally beautiful thoughts and feelings for their own religions. I wanted to know theirs and I wished to share mine. As the result of the school and as I grew older I began hiding those feelings in parts of my heart where no one could see them. I have no hate anymore, but I still dream at night, when I am by myself, that someday I could share my faith with others and not be persecuted for it."

He then looked into Verna's eyes and said, "Until now, Verna is the only one I have ever told that to. She has the same beliefs as I do in many things, but a different faith. She interprets a different meaning and she still loves me. I guess that, among other things, is why I love her so much."

James looked back at Scott, saw a big smile, and continued to look around the room and saw nothing but grins from everyone.

"Michael, I have something to tell you."

James then started to give Michael and Verna a little bit of background information of their group. And what they were doing to try and change the government by peaceful means.

Michael looked into James' eyes and said,"Why didn't you tell me before this? I thought that I was your best friend."

"You are, that's why I didn't want to involve you. If they caught me, you would have not known a thing; you would have been truly innocent."

"James, I have not been innocent since the day I went through the doors of the government reform school. I want in; I want to help your group, I want to help our people."

"Good, I will now tell you everything," James replied as they hugged each other.

*   *   *

The resistance group had long ago devised a plan to take control of Gwanameades communication array. The communications array was responsible for relaying all of the Cauldarians voice, radio and video communications for the whole planet. If it went electronically through the air, Gwanameades array was assigned to pick up the signal, boost it, and then send it back to Cauldaria. The resistance knew this relay of communications to be extremely valuable. If they could cut off the governments' information, strangle hold on the people and allow free discussion for the first time. They hoped the people of Cauldaria would start to talk and ask questions. Our group along with other dissident factions would help to expose the current governments' failures. This was the resistance's only hope, until something unexpected happened.

There was an unusual meteor shower that strangely hit Gwanameade. There were only a few major strikes against the outer rings of the space station. But one of these impact sites had something that no other live Cauldarian had ever seen. A rock, a rock that had a strange green glow, a rock that was translucent, a rock that the government said was part of the Gods of Cauldaria, something sacred, something that should be feared, something that could only be found in the forbidden spiritual zone.

Now the resistance had piece of it. It was only a rock. Just a small rock and it had no spiritual powers at all. Some of the missing and silenced Cauldarian scientist's theories would have proven to be correct. It was a green electrically charged rock.

James explained the resistance would show the people over the video array from Gwanameade the truth about the rocks in the spiritual zone and why no Cauldarian could walk into, come back out of the zone, and survive the high electrical charges in a local area that had thousands of these meteorite rocks in it.

They wanted to prove that the green glow of the spiritual zone was not of the Gods of Cauldaria, but they were made by some force, probably a greater God that they could only hope to know in their hearts, a kind God, a beautiful and understanding God. Not a God that would use fear espoused by the government. Nor, one relentlessly driven into the minds of the people, only for the purpose of control.

*   *   *

"How can I help? I'll do anything you ask of me."

"You're one of only a few here with a mind that understands the military way of thinking and you're the best pilot I've ever seen. We will need your help fighting the Archimedes. We will have to defeat her so we can transmit our information for as long as we can. We will have to defeat her so that we may awaken a sleeping giant that lie in the hearts of our people," Scott replied.

Michael looked back at Scott and said, "Archimedes who?"

18

Roads Not Taken

She stared down through the clear wall and then panned to the floor of the connecting corridor and looked upon the surface of Cauldaria. Commander Wilma Cole was used to having solid ground under her feet, not this transparent poly-glass. Even though the walkway floors had small luminous threads running across them every couple of feet, those not accustomed to walking on the translucent floor had difficulty keeping their balance, as there were few visual cues for the brain to process. Cole was not any different from anyone else, she felt slightly off balance and a little queasy. She hoped that no one would notice, especially her troops.

She was the ultimate warrior and led men and women of equal ability. They were part of a new clandestine unit not part of any of the Ministry departments. The elite shock troops she led were directly under the control of the Prime Minister. They were basically his personal troops. Under current published Cauldarian law, there was no provision or necessity for such a unit, but as with most endeavors in government, the top leaders were always, more comfortable if they had some way of suppressing societal malcontents, legally or not.

All through her career Cole was the gung-ho type and rarely asked questions or the inevitable "why" that men and women practicing the art of deadly force would eventually solicit sometime during their profession. She was a good soldier and always did her duty with no complaints to anyone, not even to her closest confidant, her husband. She always attempted to put on a staunch and stalwart appearance between and during her many tactical operations. But tonight, the commander's demeanor was different. She had a drawn look, grayish and sickly. She stood there looking down in dread holding a piece of paper in her hand. It was a communiqué from Minister Hauldan.

She wondered if she could carry out her orders to completion this time. She knew that if she did not her career was over. But these orders went against her moral code of ethics. She stood there with the realization that there was a large gray area in her ethical standards; after all, she was in the basic description of her job, a paid killer. Her only solace was she thought she had the moral high ground. And was justified in her actions. However, today she could not fit her orders in the loose gray spectrum of her principles. She was thinking of different ways of circumventing Hauldan's ludicrous commands. Her mind raced with different scenarios, all of which would get her out of this situation, but none had the foundation of truth. She would have to lie and thus lose her honor. She wondered which course she should take. The honorable one, in the states view, that would kill many innocents or the other to lie and deceive to save lives. Neither avenue appealed to her.

She crumpled the paper in her hands and let it drop. It hit the clear floor and bounced over to cover her vision of Tarwann, a coastal resort village with a population of twenty-five hundred. Knowing that by her hand, she would decide the fate of a town just as populated as Tarwann, but this one was orbiting Cauldaria and it was also inhabited by many innocent people. She wished she never read it. She suddenly hated Hauldan for putting her in such a situation.

For some reason the rarely introspective commander thought back to her time spent in university learning the ways environmental science. She once wanted to spend her life studying and working to help save the few remaining Cauldarian mammal species and their similarly important ocean bound invertebrate cousins.

She was known by her fellow students as a "bleeding heart" with an empathetic soul. Her heart was said to have always been in the right place. After many years in military service, she now asked herself if she had a heart left.

She wondered now if she had taken the right path in life, where would she be now if she had listened to her heart in her younger years and followed her love of science. For one thing, she knew she would not be standing in a corridor of Gwanameade and deciding the fate of thousands of Cauldarians. She kicked the crumpled paper to the side, looked down at Tarwann again, and walked away into the hands of providence.

19

Hope In A Little Package

The Archimedes was now only one day away. This was only one third of an elliptical orbit away from Gwanameade. Michael was being briefed on the Cauldarian war ship. He thought it strange that the government would build such a space vehicle until he studied the secret blue prints of her. Most of her weapons of mass destruction were on the underside of her hull, pointing down at Cauldaria. Her real reason for being, if needed, was to control the population of the planet.

Verna had a confidential copy of the blue prints that were sent to her for study, as she was one of Cauldaria's premier astro-engineers. Her set of plans did not include all of the structural features that would eventually be added to the orbiter.

"Verna how long has the Archimedes been operational?" Michael asked.

"Just a little longer than the Vernacaria. I had no idea of her armaments or her thick armor. I thought it was just another innocuous and expensive project sponsored by the government."

"How did they keep such a large project a secret for so long?"

James interrupted, "Only a secret to the people. The top officials of all the Ministries, the space dockworkers that built her and the resistance knew. We were going to use the Archimedes secret existence against the government, but now even her existence is paled by the discovery of the Thorellium meteorite that hit Gwanameade two days ago. The government knows it and that is why they are sending her here. They want that damn rock and they will do anything to get it."

"We have to stop the Archimedes so we can transmit our information unhindered from the hands of the government," Scott exclaimed.

"How do you know that's why she is coming here?" Verna replied.

"We intercepted some encrypted messages for the Archimedes right after we had our meteorite strikes."

"What did they say?"

Scott turned around, went over to the wall, and pushed on it lightly. His wall safe popped out from behind a holographic image of the wall. He opened the door to the safe and pulled out a crystalline memory storage module. He then inserted it into the player on his desk. The player printed out the messages, but it also had the original voice messages encrypted on it. These communiqués were from Minister Hauldan to the commander of the Archimedes. He read the last message to Michael and Verna:

Hello commander Toren, this is Minister Hauldan, this government has deemed it necessary to search the space station Gwanameade for all the samples of the meteorite strikes that occurred today. A description of these will be sent in a later communiqué. The Ministry has reason to believe these meteorites are highly dangerous and could contaminate the whole of Gwanameade. We have a few agents on the station that report there was at least one meteorite recovered. If found, DESTROY the meteorite.

For the safety of Cauldaria, if the personnel onboard Gwanameade hinder or do not allow a search of the station, you have the authority given by the Ministry to destroy and obliterate the station ring by ring until the meteorite is found or the station is no more. The troops already stationed on board Gwanameade are expendable.
End of transmission.

Scott then said, "Here is another message we just intercepted from Hauldan to the commander of the troops onboard our station. It reads:"

Commander Cole, as indicated in our previous briefing. Gwanameade is still a continuing threat to the security of Cauldaria. Continue your efforts with the airlock seals with all haste. Remember the results must look as if they were from natural causes. Our people would not understand the necessity for the stations demise.
End of transmission.

James then indicated, "Commander Cole doesn't realize Hauldan gave the commander of the

Archimedes orders to blow us up and that her troops were now considered expendable."

"We thought about giving Cole this information, but her indoctrination into the system is so complete she probably wouldn't believe us. Hauldan is going to destroy this station with her troops or with the Archimedes. He doesn't care which," Scott added.

Michael just stared ahead. Then he asked, "Where is the Archimedes and how long do I have to plan?"

James looked at a report,"She is one day away, just over the horizon. Luckily she's slow."

"Yes, but she is heavily armored and looks like a tough foe," Michael said as he looked down at the blue prints.

"Do you understand this is extremely dangerous and could cost you dearly," Scott asked.

"Yes," Michael answered, "I guess there comes a moment in most of our lives at one time or another when each of us must pledge ourselves to something greater, be it peaceful or not. My actions may well include the greatest of all sacrifices that I could give, my life."

Michael realized that tomorrow at this same time, he would most likely be dead, but hopefully he would first stop the Archimedes approach to Gwanameade.

*   *   *

Michael studied the blue prints of the Archimedes for two hours and could not find a non-defensible aspect that he and his ship the Vernacaria could take advantage. He held his head in his hands and could not believe his fate. He would be throwing his life away in a vain attempt, he was well aware that he could not even make a dent in the Archimedes armor. At least he had comfort in knowing Verna, Scott and James would be safe, as he had earlier arranged with another shuttle pilot to transport them down to Cauldaria just before the Archimedes arrived within firing range.

At his darkest moment he looked up and saw Verna standing by the window, looking out into space, the sun caressed her soft form. He wondered if she would be all right after the announcement of his almost certain death. He could already see his answer. It was falling down her face; her tears caught the golden light from the sun as they moistened her skin. He stood up, walked towards her, and reached out his arms to hug her by the warm light in the window.

He whispered into her ear, "Everything will be all right; everything will be all right my love." But he knew it wouldn't be.

While holding her tightly in his arms he could feel her little heartbeat. He remembered the first time they made love. He felt her heartbeat then too. He thought of what she whispered to him then. She told him that her little heart was the strongest thing in the universe right now, stronger than the largest sun, stronger than the biggest galaxy, her love for him could not be dwarfed by anything. She said that sometimes the most powerful things come in small packages.

Michael pulled back a few inches and looked deeply into her eyes. He could not believe it. The answers to his problems with the Archimedes could not be found in blue prints, they were to be found in Verna's heart, in her loving heart, a small lovely package that could not be stopped or overcome.

*   *   *

Michael called James and Scott to his room and began to tell them of his plans to stop the Archimedes dead in its orbit.

"I thought of this idea while talking with Verna."

"What is it?" James eagerly asked.

"I'm not going to use the Vernacaria to attack the Archimedes. I am going to use one of Gwanameades small construction shuttles. They are small, thick skinned, agile and fast."

Scott inquired, "How will you get close enough to the Archimedes to do anything and what could you do with a little one man construction shuttle? She will blow you into a million pieces if you get within gun range."

Michael smiled, "These same construction shuttles were used to construct the damn thing. The proximity security codes should still be in one of the shuttles computers. I will activate the code and the attack radar sensors won't even let the operators know I'm there, as long as they are using a tactical plot. The sensors should think I am just a repair ship, a friendly. If they haven't changed the construction proximity codes and if they are in tactical, I'll be safe."

"Those are awful big ifs." Scott replied.

He shook his head up and down, "That's all I have, and I'll need a little luck too!"

"What do you plan to do if you get close to her," James asked.

Michael snapped back, "When I get close to her, not if!"

"OK, when you get close to her," James rephrased.

"James you will be involved in this also."

"Good, I felt left out."

"You won't say that when you hear what you will have to do."

Michael looked at James as he explained, "You will have to pilot the Vernacaria, take her fast by the Archimedes. Keep their attention on you, while I'm in close they might see me visually by unaided eye, but with you zipping around they will probably miss me all together."

"But how will you disable the Archimedes?" Scott queried.

"Hell, I'm not going to disable her, I'm going to ram her up the ass and kill her."

"What!"

"The only at risk parts on the ship are the engine intakes and the engines themselves. The intakes have light armor covering them at an angle and are impossible to get through. But the engines exhaust outlets are hanging out and open. I'm going to ram her from behind and go right up her engine core."

"Do you think the construction shuttle could do it?" James asked.

"I hope so, she's just a little craft, but I'm sure she will have what it takes. I was just reminded by Verna about small packages and their power. It's our only way to succeed."

Of Green Illusions

20

Dreams

Verna and Michael decided to spend their last night together in each other's arms. There was hardly a word spoken between the two, they would spend the night making love. They had eventually fallen asleep after hours of being inseparable.

Michael had awakened first. He had the same strange dream that he had many times before. After reading, Dr. Thorensens work on the origin of the green rock and the spiritual land. His dream of where he held the Cauldarians sacred rock in his hand. His choice of whether to throw it into the night to save his people from the changes that would come from its discovery. Alternatively, the choice to expose the state sanctioned religion for what it was and how true Thorensens theory had become. He lay there thinking of what a strange dream this was. During his waking hours, his only wish was to change the government, but while sleeping and in his dreams, he had qualms about actually doing something about it.

He rolled off the bed as to not wake Verna. He wanted to make it as easy as possible for her. He went to the bathroom to wash and get clothed for his last flight. Michael turned the water on to wash the sleep from his eyes and looked down at the puddle of water growing in the sink. Looking at his reflection from the puddle of water he realized how much he had changed from the boy who dreamed about a different world to a man that was about to help change it. He wondered how he would have looked as an old man. As he stared at the reflection, he knew that he would never know.

He slipped his flight suit on, reached into his flight bag, pulled out a Cauldarian rose, and then walked back into the bedroom. He stopped halfway from the bedroom door to look at her lying in bed; she looked like a sleeping angel, one that he had always dreamed. But Verna was real, flesh and blood, a beautiful woman.

Michael walked over to the bed and quietly placed a note and the rose on the pillow next to her. Taking one of the petals off and cupping it under his eye, he captured the tears that he was crying for her. He placed the tear soaked petal next to the rose on the pillow and quietly walked to the door. As he closed the door behind him, he turned and took one last look at Verna, which is where his heart would stay.

*   *   *

He started to walk to the cafeteria for something to drink before he went to the mornings briefing. James was running towards him and yelling, "She's here; she's here!"

"Who?" Michael thought.

"The Archimedes is within firing range!"

"How the hell did she get so close, so fast?"

"They must have propulsion we don't know about."

"OK, James this means the only briefing you're going to get is on the walk to our ships. Do you have an active com link to Scott?"

"Yes."

"Good, turn it on, he will have to be in on this too."

James turned on his com link and requested to speak with commander Edwards immediately. Scott was already on duty as one of his crew had informed him of the early arrival of the Archimedes.

"Yes James, this is Scott, I was just about to contact you and Michael," He said. "Do you know the Archimedes new position?"

"Yes," Michael interrupted, "Scott, I'm going to brief you and James right now. This is going to be short because I don't have the time to be very detailed."

"That's fine."

James nodded and gave his approval as they walked to their ships. Michael then began to run down the list of actions that comprised his battle plan.

"Scott, you're going to have a tough job. You have the task of keeping Cole's troops contained and eventually subdued. If you can keep, them on the outer quarter hub of the station they will be away from the vital parts of Gwanameade and most importantly, they will be far from the communications array. Do you think you and your personnel can do it?"

"It's already done. I decided to risk talking to Cole last night. I showed her all of Hauldan's secret communiqués to date, including the message to the captain of the Archimedes indicating that Cole's troops were expendable. Her jaw dropped to the floor when she read that one. After a few minutes of silence, she admitted her troops were the ones responsible for the sabotage to the air-lock seals. She then asked how he could help our cause. I told her we would probably need her elite troops on the surface of Cauldaria to help organize the people and fight the government troops if need be."

"Well, you were busy last night--" James said with an astonished voice.

Michael interrupted. "Scott, all you will have to do now is transmit our data after James and I stop the Archimedes. Remember not to transmit until we destroy her. I don't want to provoke her captain into using his long range weapons on you."

"I Understand."

He continued, "I will keep my receiver on during my attack run, but I won't use my transmitter because they will pick that up and my position. James you will have to turn everything on. I want them to see you and to keep their eyes on you. If you have to hang your ass out the window to get their attention, do it."

James laughed, "That would surely get the Archimedes crew excited."

Michael said smilingly, "That will keep their eyes on you and will hopefully let me sneak around to her engines. We will disembark at the same time and at about half the distance to her, I want you to start the Vernacaria's quantum engines and streak close by her to get the attention of the captain. If you pass by her at a quarter of light speed your exhaust trail should still be visible, but you will be too fast for her gunners to target you. If you feel you have to accelerate faster to stay out of the gunners sights you had better do so. The speed of your sortie will be the one you are comfortable with. Remember to make your runs at oblique angles to her lateral plane; this should make it harder for her gunners. Also, stay away from the stern of the Archimedes, that's where I will be. This will be flying by the seat of your pants, improvise and remember your better than they are and faster too. Once you see explosions of any kind head back to the safety of Gwanameade."

"What about you?" James asked.

"If you see any explosions and I hope you do. It will mean my mission was successful. The only problem is, I will be expendable on this one." Michael looked down and said worryingly, "I'll be dead but, hopefully the Archimedes will be too."

*   *   *

They arrived at the dock and were about to enter the separate air locks that led to their ships. They stopped by the communications panel to say goodbye to Scott over the com system.

Michael said with a crackling voice, "Scott, you have been a dear friend and confidante; I will miss hearing your voice and your engaging laugh. I wish you were here so I could see you one last time--goodbye friend."

Michael listened for a response, but none came. He understood, it was a difficult moment for all.

James and Michael looked into each other's eyes, they each knew that they were not just best friends anymore, they were brothers, and they were going to face death together.

They unceremoniously entered their respective cockpits, fired up their engines just as they had done thousands of times before. It all seemed normal but there was a surrealistic feeling in the air. Michael's thoughts turned to Verna and wondered what part she would play in the future of Cauldaria. He could not get her image out of his head. He would relish the thoughts of her during the flight to the Archimedes.

*   *   *

Verna was startled awake by a dream that Michael, her love, was to be found dead in space. The horror of this had awakened her. Then she realized it was not a dream, it was true. He would die today.

She immediately felt for him beside her on the bed. All she found was the rose that he left her with a note that read: "Words fail me... I will love you forever..."

She glanced up through the window above her bed and saw Michael and James on the way to their destinies. She started to cry, looked down for a second, and found on Michael's pillow the liquid filled rose petal he had left for her. She held it to the window and in the starlight, it glistened, she then held it to her lips, tasted the salt of the moisture-laden petal, and knew it was her lovers' tears. She then looked back out the window at her love leaving her and flying into the dark of the night. She would weep uncontrollably for the rest of the morning.

21

A Child's Parable

After leaving Gwanameade, James and Michael separated from a formation grouping and flew on different parabolic headings. In the early stages of the attack, this pre-planned maneuver would hopefully, keep the gunners attention on James and the Vernacaria. Michael could then slip in from the other side and begin his own suicide attack run.

Michael looked out his windshield and could hardly make out the distant Vernacaria in the dark of space. He wondered what James was thinking as he piloted his ship to the dangerous rendezvous with the Archimedes. He knew James had the ability, but hoped he would make the correct choices at the right times to keep himself out of harm's way. Michael knew he was to face death in a short while, but hoped James would be spared his fate.

Michael looked in the direction of the Archimedes and could only see a faint shadow against the starry background. Out of the corner of his eye, he saw a streak of light. It was James starting his grazing runs.

He yelled through the windscreen, "NO JAMES! It's too early; they'll have time to project your trajectory. Damn! The gunners are going to pick you off."

Michael did not know the Vernacaria's sensors indicated the Archimedes was scanning the area of space that he was in and James decided to risk his own safety to protect the stealth of Michael's position.

The Archimedes did not even wait to see if James was going to transmit his flight intentions. She fired a burst of high-energy particles by his bow and another on the starboard side of the Vernacaria. Michael could see that James was flying with guile; he was flying her by hand and without the flight computers help at a quarter the speed of light.

He smiled and yelled at the Archimedes, "Yeah, he's better than you bastards! Do it James, fly her, fly her!"

The Archimedes was now getting within plain sight of Michael's little ship. James was still drawing heavy fire from the dreadnought as Michael entered the proximity codes for his little construction vehicle. The computers onboard the Archimedes must have accepted the codes, as there were no automatic inquiries from the approach control system. He breathed a sigh of relief as he passed by the outer defensive ring and was still in one piece.

He was close to her port gun positions when they opened fire and released a massive energy burst. To his surprise, it traveled past his ship. It went straight by and headed for the Vernacaria.

"Move it James! Go to full speed, full thrust! Turn her!" Michael cried out.

James could not hear his cries, but he did hear the loud explosion at the stern of the Vernacaria. He took a direct hit in the port side of the aft empennage. The old chemical engines, still installed, caught the brunt of the hit. They began to explode violently as James tried to maneuver her away from the relentless onslaught from the Archimedes. Nothing James did seemed to help; he was lost in a quagmire of deadly high-energy bursts from the large ship.

Michael just sat there and watched, flying his little ship between the two huge craft, he could do nothing; he had to continue on his attack run. He suddenly felt sick to his stomach. Not because of his own impending death, but the death of James, directly in front of his eyes and he had no way to help save him.

His sick feeling quickly turned into anger and rage. He pushed his throttles full forward, past the stops for maximum acceleration and thought to himself, if we are to die, I want to die together.

Michael took the ship off autopilot and at full thrust cut his attacking track to the stern of the Archimedes in half.

Accelerating faster and faster he yelled at the Archimedes, "For freedom, for our peoples freedom. And this is for James!"

As he approached the huge engines at full speed, something strange happened. Time seemed to slow down. Thoughts ran through his mind. Thoughts of his parents and his boyhood drifted through his consciousness. Good and warm thoughts, happiness now invaded every second. He thought of Verna and the wonderful times they had together.

As he entered the plume of the Archimedes engines and watched the flames engulf his windshield. He thought of a passage from a children's parable that his mother read to him as a child:

Where are you going child
Where are you now
Bear the chapter open

Bear the world to come about
Open the pages or none adrift will be found
Through your heart
The way lies open
Pray the path be found
Bear the chapter open
You will turn the world around ....

Just as he went through the song in his thoughts and in this strange state of being, he now realized the full extent of his sacrifice. He was now prepared to die.

His little ship was now seconds away from melting and from impacting into the Archimedes huge engine core. Michael felt a sudden jolt. He wondered what it was. Then everything went black...

*   *   *

All of the little construction vehicles had a long forgotten safety feature. In case of collision during construction, the crew compartment was to be ejected rearward to save the crew. This feature was automatic and was out of the control of the crews flying them. None had ever crashed and so the ejection mechanism was never used and was eventually forgotten.

Michael blacked out from the high negative G forces induced from the ejection sequence. He awakened moments later to see the Archimedes drifting in space. Her impregnable thick armor was buffeting from internal explosions and looked like thin paper blowing in the wind. The skin rippled and burst open in violent bursts of energy. Her exploding engine core was about to break the massive ship apart. The energy gun arrays started to implode and then in one last fireball she lost all form. She blew into a billion pieces. The Archimedes was dead.

Michael could not believe what he saw. He felt elated, he was alive and the Archimedes was obliterated. He gathered his wits and then realized, James, where's James? As he looked in the general direction of James last position, he heard Scott's voice over the communications panel. It was on an open channel. An open channel! Gwanameade was now transmitting on all radio, video and data channels freely with no government control. The Cauldarian people were now receiving uncensored information on the current government and its sacred spiritual zone. They were receiving information on the genuine origins of the government's power base, the control of their hearts and minds through a state enforced religion that was based upon fear and a simple green rock.

As Michael listened to Scott broadcasting unhindered to their world of Cauldaria he had tears in his eyes, because he found James. He saw a burning hunk of metal floating by. It was the

Vernacaria. James was dead. He just stared at it, wiping the tears from his eyes. His friend was gone.

Michael thought what a high price to pay for freedom.

*   *   *

After many months of political upheaval on Cauldaria the government that Michael grew up to know and have such disdain for was no more. A new form of government replaced Hauldan and his Ministries. The Cauldarian people could actually cast their vote in real elections now and have a say in their future. True choice was a strange and unusual concept for them. It would be a long process and would take years for the Cauldarians to form a fully representative government, but the people were now finding out how to think for themselves, govern themselves, and most importantly learn how to follow their own hearts in discovering their own beliefs. The many Ministries fell one by one. There were those that still believed in the old system; it was all they knew. Even with all the newly exposed information there was a hardcore group unwilling to give up their power base and continued to look to Keiods religion for guidance. Eventually, time and the open society that was fought for proved to work against the holdouts of the old regime.

Everyone that observed the political arena and knew when Hauldan stepped down there was more than a good chance that religious and political freedom was not only possible it was now inevitable in the future lives of all Cauldarians.

*   *   *

On warm summer nights, Michael and Verna would stand hand in hand on the little hill where he had first felt the touch of God. They would stand there looking into the starry night and wonder at the spectacle of the universe that lay before them. They would also think of James on these nights, he would be in their hearts forever.

They would stand hand in hand under summer night skies for many years to come....